Gwen bounced into the room. "Alec, look!"

Alec's mouth went dry. He swallowed, or tried to. "You look tasty...." He trailed off with a gesture. "I mean, tasteful."

"Well, tasteful wasn't quite the look I was going for, but with this V-neck, I figured the 'Wonder Bra' would be overkill." Gwen pushed her arms together and manufactured an impressive cleavage. "I don't know—what do you think? To cleave, or not to cleave?"

Think? She expected him to think? "Uhhh..."

"Yeah, you're right." She released her breasts and gestured to her skirt. "So how about the skirt?"

With difficulty, Alec transferred his gaze to the black skirt she was wearing. It was just a skirt, not particularly short or tight...except that it *did* cling ever so nicely. He peered closer. Was it see-through, or was he just imagining her legs? The more he stared, the better it looked. The better *she* looked.

He was in such trouble.

D0720701

Dear Reader,

Secret man-magnets? Why not? You and I both know they're out there. Some women have them—and some women don't. That can be the only possible explanation why there are so many fabulous—yet dateless—women out there. Not that the dating women aren't fabulous, too, but this book wasn't written for them. No, this book is for the single woman—a woman like Gwen, who comes into possession of a skirt that brings men to their knees...and discovers she can't fit into it! But her mother can.... So, she pretends it doesn't matter because she's given up on men, even though she's awfully tempted by the perfect man who'd only need the *slightest* nudge to notice her. And wouldn't the skirt come in handy? Only, her mother's already wearing it...and attracting all the men! Don't you hate when that happens?

Whether you're dating or not, I hope you enjoy the further adventures of the SINGLE IN THE CITY women you first met in Cara Summer's *Moonstruck in Manhattan*. And don't miss the skirt's next challenge in Kristin Gabriel's *Seduced in Seattle*, available next month.

Enjoy,

Heather MacAllister

P.S. Stop by www.HeatherMacAllister.com for more SINGLE IN THE CITY news!

TEMPTED IN TEXAS
Heather MacAllister

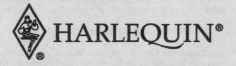

HARLEQUIN®

TORONTO • NEW YORK • LONDON
AMSTERDAM • PARIS • SYDNEY • HAMBURG
STOCKHOLM • ATHENS • TOKYO • MILAN • MADRID
PRAGUE • WARSAW • BUDAPEST • AUCKLAND

To Shirley Rose Kraus
and Kay LaBauve Parnell
with Alpha Gam love

ISBN 0-373-25964-6

TEMPTED IN TEXAS

Copyright © 2002 by Heather W. MacAllister.

Visit us at www.eHarlequin.com

Printed in U.S.A.

Prologue

"THAT SAPPY LOOK is back on your face." Gwen Kempner spoke through her teeth in order to maintain her bridesmaid's smile—fake, but definitely not sappy. It's not that she wasn't happy for the bride; it's that her happiness was grounded in a thorough knowledge of male-female relationships.

Unsuccessful ones, as it happened. Therefore, she felt no mawkish sentimentality when it came to weddings and happily ever afters. Or even happily ever afters without weddings.

Kate, her best friend and fellow bridesmaid, sighed dreamily. "Just look at her, Gwen."

Gwen dutifully looked toward Chelsea, her other best friend, who had an equally sappy look on her face as she gazed adoringly at Zach, her new husband. Gwen decided she could spot Chelsea a sappy look or two—after all, she was the bride.

"She looks so beautiful," Kate cooed.

Oh, no. Kate was going over to the dark side. Gwen shot her a sharp look.

"Now, Kate, we've talked about this. Brides look that way because they develop a special immunity to reality. They have to in order to justify the hideous cost of a dress they'll only wear once. It wears off after they pay the 'heirlooming' bill from the dry cleaners."

"But she looks so happy, Gwen. Maybe—"

"Be strong and repeat after me...I do not need a man to be happy."

"I don't know—did you check out the best man?"

"Of course I did. Then I imagined making beer runs for the best man and all his ex-jock friends who spend every weekend during football season reliving past glories in front of a big-screen TV he's squeezed into my living room—and I get over it."

"You miss the big-screen TV. Admit it."

Kate was referring to Gwen's last serious relationship in which she'd had to move out of her apartment in order to break up because her ex refused to move his TV, exercise equipment and stereo. She'd even abandoned her couch, which had sustained severe nacho cheese damage. Since she'd moved out on a Super Bowl Sunday he hadn't noticed until the next day.

Kate clutched her arm. "Look! She's going to throw the bouquet!"

"Thanks for the warning." Gwen edged backward into the crowd of poor, deluded females who surrounded them.

"Oh, no, you don't!" Kate pulled her back to the front.

Gwen stumbled forward at the precise moment Chelsea threw the bouquet. Kate, the traitor, dropped her arm to grab for it, and Gwen fell to her knees.

The bouquet sailed over her head. There was a squeal followed by a very unladylike scuffle.

Gwen picked herself up in time to meet Chelsea's eyes.

And froze. In her hands, Chelsea held something far more deadly than a mere bridal bouquet.

"Not the skirt!"

Chelsea hefted the black fabric and before Gwen realized she was about to throw, flung it, Frisbee-style, right toward her.

Gwen automatically held up her arms to fend off the skirt and it caught on her hand, then draped itself over her head, clinging as though glued.

"No!"

"Gwen, you've caught the skirt, you lucky thing." Kate's voice sounded behind her as Gwen snatched the skirt off her head. "And here I was going for the bouquet."

"Wanna trade?"

"Sure, but we can't. You know the rules."

"Rules? There are no rules."

"Yes, there are. You caught it, you wear it. If you don't, it's like breaking a chain letter or something."

"Kate, we're talking about a *skirt*."

"And not just any skirt."

"Yes! That's exactly what it is—just a skirt."

"If you can refer to a skirt that has been responsible for two women finding the men of their dreams as 'just a skirt,' then okay. Me, I'm a believer."

Gwen groaned. "Not the magical power thing. Torrie just made that up. Come on, Kate."

An unnatural quiet had descended on the group of single women who'd gathered to try to catch the bouquet. They were avidly soaking up every word.

"Is that it? The skirt Torrie said came from the island? Can I touch it?" one asked.

Someone else must have asked Kate to explain, because she immediately launched into the tale Torrie, their friend from school, had told everyone about how the women of an island spun a fabric made from a special thread. The fabric when given to a young woman of marriageable age, was guaranteed to attract her one true love. The crowd breathed a collective "oooh."

"Yeah—I read about it in a magazine," someone said.

What was the matter with them?

"Ladies!" Gwen snapped her fingers. "We're in the twenty-first century here!"

They ignored her in favor of Kate, who was actually *encouraging* them. "...and it's being passed from bride to bride."

Calculating eyes turned to Gwen. "So go put it on," someone suggested.

"Yeah. Quit wasting time," someone else said to agreeing murmurs.

"Use the bride's dressing room." Kate had a look in her eyes that Gwen had never seen before. "Don't make me wait too long for my turn."

"Stop."

Everyone looked toward a thirtyish woman. "If that thing's a man magnet, then you will all understand if I remove my fiancé from the scene?"

"I don't believe this," Gwen murmured, but nobody heard her. They were too busy gathering their own significant others and spiriting them away from Gwen's new irresistibility.

"Come on, Gwen." Kate was urging her toward the

changing room. "I hear the band's booked for another hour and Chelsea's cute cousin isn't married."

"Kate!" Gwen stared. "Look, I don't want this thing. You take it." She wadded up the fabric and tried to fling it toward her friend.

"Ow!" Her hands and arm stung. Startled, she looked down, expecting to see a red rash or something. Nothing showed, but the painful tingle continued.

"What's the matter?" Kate asked.

"I don't know. Maybe I'm allergic to slinky fabric. Either that or a spider or some equally disgusting creature has stung me."

"Oh, ick!" Kate backed away.

Gwen shook out the skirt. As she did so, the subdued light caught the fabric, giving it a rich luster.

Fingering it, she noted the thick, sumptuous feel. The fabric was quality stuff. She held it up to herself and the length hovered near her knees. Not too short and not dowdily long, either.

She didn't have so many clothes that she could just fling away a classy, basic, black skirt.

"Maybe I'll keep it after all," she said to Kate.

But Kate and the other guests were flowing toward the door of the penthouse, passing by two little girls who held baskets of pastel froth.

Treating the skirt with more respect, Gwen folded it and draped it over her arm. The burning and tingling had completely stopped and the skirt swayed against her arm in a sensuous ripple—almost a caress.

How weird was that?

Weird enough to give her the creeps.

Hurrying to catch up with Kate, Gwen stopped and

took a net bag of birdseed to throw at Chelsea and Zach, thinking that people sure threw a lot of stuff at weddings.

Once everyone made it down to the building lobby, Kate gestured for Gwen to come stand right beside the getaway car. Bad move, because they got hit with as much birdseed as Chelsea did.

Chelsea got into the car, dragging her dress in after her. Laughing, she waved goodbye. "Just think—the next time we get together, it'll be for Gwen's wedding!"

Gwen tacked on her bridesmaid smile and waved. If that's what they thought, then the three of them wouldn't be together again for a long, long time.

"LET ME GET THIS STRAIGHT—the bride threw you a skirt that has special man-attracting powers?"

Gwen hefted her suitcase into the trunk of her friend's car. "That she *claims* has special man-attracting powers. And not just any man, but supposedly your one, true love. There've even been articles written about it. Isn't that a hoot?" she prompted when Laurie didn't roll her eyes or fall over laughing.

"I think it's sweet."

Sweet? Gwen had felt the need to talk to a rational, nonwedding-infected female. Laurie VanCamp, a friend from work who was giving her a ride home from the airport, was just the person. Or so Gwen had thought.

But Laurie wasn't scoffing the way she was supposed to. "Tell me the whole story again."

So Gwen did as they left Houston's Bush Airport, merged onto the freeway and headed for Gwen's apartment in the Galleria area. By the time Laurie matched speed with the other cars barreling down the freeway, Gwen was sorry she'd told her anything.

"What's the skirt look like?" Laurie asked.

"Black, slinky but classy, knee-length—nothing special."

"Has it been road-tested?"

"Sort of."

"Has it or hasn't it?"

Sheesh. "Yeah, I suppose."

"Well, does it work?" Laurie was taking this whole thing way too seriously.

"How should I know?" Gwen snapped.

"How many of the women found their husbands while wearing it?" Laurie asked with exaggerated patience.

Gwen sighed. "Both of them," she admitted.

Laurie shot her a startled look, then trained her eyes back on the highway. "And your problem with this skirt is...?"

"Aside from not believing a word of the story? I don't want a man."

"Right."

"Really! Men take too much time and energy. And they're unreliable. I mean, look—you had to come get me at the airport because the guy changing the oil in my car didn't have it ready when he said he would."

"The last Sunday in December is prime football playoff season, not to mention all the college bowl games. What do you expect?"

"I expect him to do what he said he would! I should have known better, but the fact that he's my neighbor made me forget he's a man."

"He's doing you a favor—give him a break."

"I'm *paying* him. And why are you making excuses for him? I was stranded at the airport and he'd had three days to change the oil. You shouldn't have had to mess up your Sunday afternoon just so he could watch football." She shook her head. "I don't need the aggravation. Men are like a really time-consuming hobby that's become more trouble than it's worth. I'll be better off concentrating on my career."

"Like the world needs more caffeine."

"Hey! You work at Kwik Koffee, too!"

"Yes, but if you're giving up men, it should be for something noble like finding a cure for cancer or heart disease or becoming an astronaut or something."

"You see? You see? You just proved my point. More women would have those careers if they didn't have to spend their time catering to men."

"So find a man who isn't a jerk like Eric."

Like that was so easy. "I didn't *know* Eric was a jerk when we started going out." She gritted her teeth to keep from listing all his jerkish traits for about the eleven millionth time.

"And you're still letting him yank your chain. Gwen, honey, it's time to move on."

"I have. By—my—self. Seriously. I'm through with men. Don't need 'em."

"Sure you do." Laurie gave her an infuriating smile.

"Why? I've got a job, a nice apartment, a pair of Jimmy Choo shoes and a vibrator—why do I need a man?"

Laurie snickered. "Uh…companionship?"

"I'll make a note to myself to get a dog—they're not as much trouble."

"Okay, then…" Laurie drew herself up, physically preparing to deliver the coup de grâce to the conversation. "Children." She sat back and waited for Gwen's reaction.

"They take longer to housebreak than dogs. And men."

"Such cynicism does not become you." Laurie signaled and took the Westheimer exit off the 610 loop.

"Sure it does. I've practiced a world-weary expression that makes me look attractively sophisticated." Gwen demonstrated.

Stopping at the traffic light gave Laurie time to study her. "You'll get wrinkles."

"That's what Botox injections are for."

Laurie looked disgusted—an expression that Gwen couldn't help noticing would give *her* frown lines. She decided not to mention it.

"So you're not going to wear the skirt."

The skirt again. "Oh, I'll wear it. I'm just not going to go manhunting in it."

"I can't believe you're being so selfish. You said your friend, Kate, has to catch it after you, if she's still single. But after her, it'll be a free-for-all grab and I want an invitation to *that* wedding."

"You're that desperate for a man?"

"As I understand it, the skirt attracts lots of men before true love wins out. What fun." Laurie sighed.

What had happened to the independent, competent, take-no-prisoners Laurie she worked with? "Our foremothers would be appalled to hear this conversation. *Your* mother would be appalled to hear this conversation. What about all the struggling, protesting and fighting for equal rights, and burning bras—"

"Like that did anything but give them sagging boobs."

"—so their daughters—we—could have a choice in how we live our lives?"

Laurie shrugged and turned into Gwen's apartment complex. "So I'm choosing to live it with a man."

"And I'm choosing not to."

Laurie slid a look at her. "You've done a real good job of getting the word out, because I haven't noticed that many men around that you could choose not to have a life with."

Gwen bristled. "Then you haven't been looking."

"Really? When was the last time a man asked you for a date?"

"Well, I—"

"Not business-related, just you and an eligible man—meaning he's single, uninvolved, straight and looking."

"Looking for what?"

"Involvement at some level."

"Does superficial involvement count?" Gwen asked cynically.

"In your case, yes. So when?"

Gwen smiled in triumph. "Remember Paddy O'Brien's cousin?"

"The Paddy O'Brien who owns the Shamrock pub?"

Gwen nodded. "When his cousin was visiting from Ireland over St. Patrick's Day, Paddy set us up for the green beer party."

Laurie was silent a moment. "You can't get much more superficial than that."

"Hey!"

"Even allowing for blind dates—"

"It wasn't a blind date. He was working the bar

when we stopped in earlier that week. Remember those Irish coffees?"

"Oh, yeah."

"Is that all you can say? You had three."

"And haven't had another since." Laurie managed to find a parking space across the alley drive from Gwen's apartment. She parked, then leveled a look at her. "You're counting hanging around a guy during a green beer party as a date?"

"Sure am."

"But he didn't take you anywhere, spend any money on you and you certainly weren't alone, not to mention the possibility that he might have had an Irish colleen stashed away in the motherland, which I guess really doesn't matter because you never saw him again."

Gwen sighed. "No muss, no fuss. Perfect, wasn't he?"

"But Gwen...how can you not want to date anybody?"

"Because dating leads to relationships."

"You wish."

"No, I *don't* wish. My life is just fine the way it is, thank you very much. And you should be encouraging me. I've recognized the pattern of my mistakes and I'm trying to break the cycle."

"But breaking the cycle doesn't mean giving up *all* men—just the wrong ones."

Gwen threw up her hands. "But I can't seem to figure out how to avoid the wrong ones until it's too late!"

"Isn't that what the skirt's for?"

Gwen rolled her eyes. "Forget the skirt."

"I don't want to forget the skirt. Things have

changed since the last time you swam a few laps in the dating pool."

"Men have stopped being self-centered?"

"That's an attractive self-confidence."

"Do they still act like they're at an all-you-want sex buffet?"

"More and more are into à la carte."

"From the same menu? For ever and ever?"

"You just came back from a wedding!"

"And most important—will they share dessert?"

Laurie gave her a puzzled look. "I've lost the analogy."

Gwen wasn't surprised. "Relationships require give and take and I got tired of being the one doing all the giving. I keep promising myself that each time will be different and then..." She shrugged. "So no more men."

"Okay, fine. Just wear the skirt until some guy asks you out, then pass it on to another deserving woman before you reject him."

"It's supposed to be thrown at a wedding, remember? Kate has to have it next."

Laurie grinned. "And I'd be happy to take it to her. Let me see it before you go."

"Whatever."

They both got out of the car and Gwen shrugged out of her coat, grateful for the mild Texas weather after frigid New York. Laurie opened the trunk and Gwen unzipped her suitcase. The skirt was right on top.

Laurie reached for the folded skirt and shook it out. "It's just a black skirt," she said with disappointment. "I wonder why men are attracted to it." She eyed

Gwen speculatively. "Wear it to my New Year's Eve party. We'll test it then."

"I didn't know you were having a New Year's Eve party."

"Neither did I. I feel strangely compelled."

"Give me that." Gwen snatched the skirt away and put it back into her suitcase.

"I'm still having the party."

"Everyone's already got plans."

"Do you have plans?" Laurie asked.

"Well, I usually go over to my parents'...stop looking at me like that!" Gwen dragged her suitcase out of Laurie's car.

"How am I supposed to look at you? It sounds so pathetic!"

"It's not! They have an open house—and an open bar, the good stuff. It's not a jug wine-and-chips kind of thing. And they serve real champagne at midnight," she added with a touch of desperation when Laurie continued to look at her with deepening pity. "And it can't hurt my career to network with their friends."

Laurie squinted into the distance. "Their friends could have sons." She nodded. "Could be good. I'll come, too."

"You're not invited!"

"Why not?"

"What about your party?"

She waved her hand. "Everyone will already have plans."

"You aren't going to find any men there—at least not men our age. They're my *parents'* friends."

"I can't be your parents' friend?"

Her mother *had* breezily suggested Gwen bring "somebody." Gwen knew she had meant somebody male, somebody to deflect the annual marital status grilling. She eyed Laurie. Bringing a female might be even better. Definitely better. There would never again be any of those "When are you...?" questions.

"Okay," she said.

"Great! Can I bring anything?"

"No. It's catered. Oh, and I always sleep over, so pack your jammies."

"Ooo, not jammies. What if someone sees me?"

Laurie was blond, young and in good shape. Very good shape. She'd blow out the men's pacemakers. "Bring a robe."

"No, no, no, no, no. You misunderstood. I might want to be seen."

"I understood all right. It's flannel and opaque or you don't go."

Laurie threw out her lower lip in a pout. "That's not very festive."

"It's a New Year's Eve party at my parents' place. You aren't supposed to be festive!"

Laurie raised an eyebrow.

"Not festive in that way," Gwen said.

"You mean in a prepared-for-serendipity way?"

"I mean in a going-after-middle-aged-married-men way."

"You should talk. You're the one who's going to be wearing the skirt. You'll see. And so will their wives. But don't worry. I'll be there to watch your back."

Gwen shuddered at the thought. "We'll talk about it tomorrow," she said noncommittally and began wheeling her suitcase over to the covered parking. "Thanks for the ride." She turned to wave at Laurie and nearly smacked her in the face because she was right behind her. "What are you doing?"

Laurie discreetly pointed to Gwen's charcoal gray Japanese import. "Are those legs supposed to be under your car?"

Gwen had already seen the cutoff clad legs of her neighbor sticking out from beneath her car. He'd driven over the curb so that the front wheels were lifted off the ground. From the angle they now stood, she could see under the car to the slice of well-muscled midriff that was also exposed. She heaved a deep breath in irritation. "Yeah."

Laurie audibly swallowed. "You don't need the skirt. Give it to me right now."

Clearly, Laurie wasn't going anywhere without an introduction. Even though Gwen had given up men, she still didn't want to see her neighbor's reaction to Laurie in hunting mode. She had a nice little nonrelationship thing going with him and Laurie could really screw it up.

Honestly, Gwen didn't know how she did it, yet right now, she could feel Laurie getting into the zone. It was more than just throwing back her shoulders and licking her lips. Something about her walk changed. And her expression. She made eye contact with a vengeance.

Just for the sake of experimentation, Gwen tried making eye contact with her neighbor's legs. It didn't work—and not only because he chose that moment to shove himself from beneath the car and stretch, providing them with a brief, yet highly memorable view of his supine body.

Gwen choked in the middle of swallowing.

"Hey, Gwen, you're back!" Shoving himself off the stained pavement, he brushed at the back of his shorts, examined his hands, reached for a red rag and wiped them off.

"Hi, Alec. This is..."

But Laurie was ahead of her purring, "Hi. I'm Laurie."

"Laurie, this is my neighbor, Alec Fleming," Gwen said at the same moment Alec was reaching for Laurie's hand and introducing himself.

Clearly her work here was done. Ordinarily, Gwen would discreetly move away, but she wanted to see the show. And there was the matter of knowing whether or not Alec was finished with her car.

Laurie immediately moved closer to him, getting into his personal space, Gwen noted, though she didn't know why she bothered. She wasn't planning on using any of Laurie's stalking tips.

Alec had tucked his fingertips in his back pockets, a pose that displayed the width of his chest and showed off his arms, which were revealed by a sweatshirt that he'd cut the sleeves off. The ragged edges emphasized his shoulders.

Ah, mating rituals. Laurie looked dazzled and not as sure of herself as she usually did.

Gwen could see why. Even in his grease-monkey state—or maybe *because* of his grease-monkey state—Alec was looking mighty fine.

But then, he usually did. He was lucky enough to

have a natural honey-on-whole-wheat-toast color of skin that meant he looked good without subjecting himself to the damaging effects of the sun.

Now that she'd given up men, Gwen would no longer be subjecting herself to multihour sessions involving exfoliation and painting her body with self-tanner, then standing with outstretched arms during most of a movie-of-the-week and hoping that no one was peeking through the space where her curtains didn't quite meet.

Men. Too much trouble. She shook her head slightly as Laurie wrinkled her nose. *Wrinkled her nose.* Someone probably once told her it looked cute. Gwen supposed it did, in a way, if you were a man. *Look at me. I'm so helpless and you're so big and strong.* Ick, ick and more ick.

"I really appreciate you giving Gwen, here, a ride home." Alec turned just enough to include Gwen in their charmed circle.

"Gwen's a friend. I didn't mind," Laurie breathed.

At least she didn't tell him it hadn't been any trouble, because *any* trip to the busy Houston airport was a royal pain.

"And aren't you just the sweetest thing to change her oil for her?"

Laurie's voice had taken a syrupy tone to which she wasn't entitled since she'd been born and raised in Kansas City. Gwen narrowed her eyes at her, but she didn't notice.

Alec didn't either. He was too busy flashing a grin at Laurie. "She's paying me!"

Which was what Gwen had already told her. It mollified her somewhat that Alec admitted it. She was about to complain about her car not being ready when he continued.

"And I've earned every penny." He lowered his brows—attractively—at her in mock sternness. "Lady, when's the last time you had your oil changed? The filter was frozen in there."

Gwen suddenly found herself on the defensive. "I, uh..."

"Since you've chosen *not* to buy American, I needed to borrow a metric tool set, which I didn't realize I'd need until *after* I'd drained all the oil out." He rubbed his index finger against a spot above his eyebrow, leaving a faint smudge that detracted not one whit from his appearance.

"Shame on you, Gwen," Laurie said snidely.

Gwen glared at her until Laurie remembered they weren't in competition for Alec's attention.

"But I'm probably just as bad about car maintenance." Which was a lie. Laurie was a fanatic about car maintenance because she'd once been stranded in the middle of the night after going to a trendy new club in an iffy area of Houston and never wanted to repeat the experience. However, Gwen understood that Laurie was trying to make up for her earlier comment.

"It was poor planning on my part, I'll admit. My brother-in-law wouldn't bring me his tools until half-time. Texas is playing Penn State," Alec added.

"Oh, yeah," Gwen said, as though she followed college football. After Eric, she'd had enough of football.

"Like I said, it wasn't a problem." Laurie was still hanging around and Gwen guessed she was giving

Alec a chance to say something along the lines of "Let me buy you dinner to make it up to you."

He wouldn't, Gwen figured. Alec Fleming was starting his own business and currently had no money. Gwen suspected that he might have once had—he'd made a reference or two about working at a family business—but he didn't have any money now, which was why he'd offered to change her oil instead of Gwen going to the quick oil-change place she usually did.

"So is the car finished?" she asked.

"At last." He looked skyward.

Hiding her smile, Gwen dug in her shoulder bag. "I am *not* going to pay you extra."

"What? No tip?"

"Sure, I'll give you a tip." She nodded to his outfit. "Wear warmer clothes when you go outside to play." She handed him a ten-dollar bill.

"I'm not cold. Besides, they're all dirty." He snapped the bill, held it up the light, then kissed it. "Laundry money!"

As they laughed, Gwen glanced at Laurie. Her expression, formerly interested and encouraging, had done a complete one-eighty. Gwen followed her gaze back to Alec and she understood. Instead of an eligible potential boyfriend, Laurie was now seeing him as a good-looking, but broke, mechanic with no ambition and no prospects.

Gwen smiled faintly. Like most women her age, she had one of those in her background and while they were fun, once was enough.

Alec wasn't anything of the sort and if Laurie asked,

Gwen would tell her. Could she help it if Laurie wouldn't ask?

"Time for me to get going," Laurie said. "Great meeting you." She gave a tight nod to Alec. To Gwen, she said, "I'll call you."

Gwen noticed that Alec stopped making love to his ten-dollar bill long enough to watch Laurie walk off.

"Nice," he said, and Laurie hadn't even put anything extra in her walk.

"Yes."

"But out of my price range."

"What do you mean by that?"

At her sharp tone, he turned to her. A second later, realization dawned. "No! Hey—I just meant that a woman like that is high-maintenance and expensive. To stay in the running you've got to take her to clubs and restaurants and the bill runs up real quick...and I'm just digging myself deeper into a hole, aren't I?" He gave her a charmingly rueful grin. Alec had charm to spare and knew it.

"Any deeper and there'll be an echo."

He held up both hands, black-creased palms outward. "I meant nothing against your friend."

"I know. It's okay." Gwen agreed with him, anyway, but wouldn't betray the sisterhood by admitting it.

"And, ah, I didn't mean that you weren't worth running up the tab for, either."

She wished he hadn't said that. They both knew she wasn't a Laurie type and honestly, Gwen was all for the Lauries of this world. Why shouldn't they value themselves enough to require men to make an effort? For all the effort Gwen required, she was a bigger bargain than a Christmas sweater in January. She needed to stop that.

But she didn't want to have that kind of discussion with Alec, who was still standing there, searching her face for a sign of whether she was mad at him or not. He was a decent, if typically male, sort.

"I'm in a good position to guilt you into a really expensive evening, aren't I?"

He didn't smile and Gwen felt a twinge of that same guilt for making him suffer. But just a twinge. "Let me have a moment to savor the feeling...." She drew a deep breath. "I'm done. You're off the hook."

He grinned and his whole stance relaxed. "You're okay, Gwen." He made a movement and for a second, she thought he was going to give her a punch on the arm, but at the last minute, he swung his hand upward and raked his fingers through his hair. "Hey, you should give your car a spin around the block to make sure it's running okay. Or I could do it for you," he added casually.

He probably had errands to run. She really didn't mind, though she was succumbing to his charm more than she should.

"Would you?" Gwen asked, as though he'd be doing her a huge favor.

"Sure!" He patted his shorts for her keys and dug them out. "I might stop off at the grocery store and get some quarters. Need anything?"

Gwen shook her head.

"Uh—do I look okay? I don't have a grease moustache, or anything?"

"Just..." She hesitated, then reached up and rubbed

at the faint streak on his brow bone. She could feel him watching her and hoped she wouldn't do anything horridly juvenile like blush.

He had warm brown hair and warm—friendly warm—brown eyes to go with his warm brown body. Okay, so the warm body part was a wild guess based solely on his forehead, but the rest was true. Gwen also had brown hair and eyes, but her hair wasn't as rich as his since she'd quit streaking it. What was the point? She'd given up men.

Funny how she had to keep reminding herself.

Especially when she was around Alec.

2

MAYBE IT WAS being around Chelsea and Kate and the wedding, or maybe it *was* the skirt—or more likely Alec and his stupid cutoffs—but Gwen decided she needed to do something active to remind her of her goals.

Or at least fine-tune them a bit. As she unpacked her suitcase, Gwen reflected on what Laurie had said about the intrinsic value of playing caffeine fairy to the office workers in the greater Houston area. In the mornings when people arrived at their jobs after fighting the rush-hour traffic and were absolutely dying for that first cup of coffee, the Kwik Koffee machines were mighty important. And didn't those cardiologists and astronauts and scientists drink coffee, coffee that her company made sure was fresh, hot and available? Didn't it put them in the right frame of mind to begin their days of important discoveries and saving lives? Therefore, wasn't Gwen actually helping the world?

Okay, so that was a stretch, but she'd file it away for the next time Laurie downplayed their importance in the grand scheme of things.

But she'd also realized that climbing up the ladder at her company was really only a means to her true goal: she, Gwen Kempner, wanted to live the life of a man. Not *be* a man, just get the same advantages.

From where she stood—currently on a chair so she could shove her suitcase onto the top shelf of her closet—men had it pretty good and that was because they had conned women into helping them. They didn't even have to be married—Gwen had noticed that the single men always seemed to have a girlfriend or even a spare mother to take care of them or wait for various delivery people. Men could even negotiate the after-five delivery times, whereas Gwen always got the, "Don't you have a neighbor who's home during the day?" question. Once, and she wasn't proud of this, she'd taken half a personal day to wait for the cable guy for Eric.

Never again.

She needed somebody to help her, someone to take care of the little things so she didn't have to.

She needed a wife.

Most career women did, and since they couldn't have one, the superachievers who could afford to hired nannies, housekeepers and personal assistants. Gwen didn't need a nanny, and she didn't mind cleaning her apartment herself. But boy howdy, a personal assistant was sure looking good. The trick was to get the company to pay for one and they weren't going to pay for a junior member of the regional director's staff to have an assistant.

So Gwen would just have to become a regional director.

After sorting the clothes she was going to take to the dry cleaners tomorrow, Gwen looked again at the skirt.

No washing instructions. In fact, no label of any kind. She couldn't exactly call Chelsea on her honeymoon and ask her how the thing was supposed to be cleaned. The skirt looked fine and Gwen decided that Chelsea had cleaned it before she'd passed it on.

Okay, then. Gwen hung it up, got out her laptop, plugged it into the phone line, flipped on the TV and proceeded to check her office e-mail. She'd missed work Friday and it would pay to get a jump on the week instead of spending Monday morning getting up to speed. That's what people who wanted promotions did.

Assuming there were no coffee crises requiring her immediate attention, she'd spend the rest of the evening coming up with a battle plan that would lead to a promotion. After all, the sooner she got an assistant, the better.

ALEC STUDIED all the laundry detergents and picked the cheapest no-name brand he could find. Passing up fabric softeners—a luxury he hadn't missed—he headed for the frozen food aisle to see if there were any ninety-nine cent TV dinners or frozen pot pies on sale three for a dollar.

Instead, he found himself tempted by store-brand frozen pizzas. They weren't big, but they were three for five dollars. However, right next to them—at two for five dollars—he found a more generously sized-and-topped brand. Before he could talk himself out of it, he'd grabbed the pizza and then had the insane impulse to buy a six-pack of domestic beer. His import days were gone for now. Unfortunately, as he stood in front of the cooler, he realized that even a six-pack was out of the question, so he snagged two oversize individual bottles and made his way toward the express checkout lane.

What are you doing? It was the voice of reason, which had been remarkably silent when he'd accepted his grandfather's gleeful challenge, but which could always be counted on to provide wet-blanket thoughts every time Alec contemplated anything that might be self-indulgent these days.

But Alec knew what he was doing. He'd already done the math and would have enough quarters left for three loads of laundry, though only enough to dry two.

So he'd dredge up fifty cents from somewhere or hang his jeans over the kitchen chairs for a couple of days. No big deal.

Besides stranding Gwen at the airport, he was conscious of having hurt her feelings. Maybe hurt was too strong a word because Gwen didn't seem the overly sensitive sort and they didn't have that kind of relationship. But he felt a gesture was called for because he liked Gwen. He counted her as his first woman friend. Not a former girlfriend from whom he'd parted amicably and still ran into from time to time, but a person he'd met and come to know since he'd lived in the apartment on Westheimer. In fact, he thought of her as a person first and a woman after that—if at all—which was why he'd spoken without thinking.

Somehow, they'd skipped all the messy girl-boy stuff and were just casual friends. He was pretty sure she wasn't currently seeing anyone, though he hardly tracked her every move. He did know that she worked a lot of overtime, but then, so did he.

In fact, he worked all the time. He had a nifty, no-brainer, thirty-hour-a-week job as the clerk in a pager store that was within walking distance of his apartment. The rest of the time he spent trying to get his fledgling business off the ground.

But tonight, he would give it a rest.

Alec handed the grocery clerk the ten-dollar bill, asked for his change in quarters, then shoved them into his pocket, noting a grease smudge on his arm as he did so.

He'd changed the oil in a car. A self-satisfied smile creased his face as he walked toward Gwen's car in the parking lot. He'd never changed oil before. Just to be on the safe side, he checked under Gwen's car for any ominous puddles.

Nope. All right!

He'd spent way too much time and had called his brother-in-law three times, but he'd done it—unfortunately, not in time to pick up Gwen from the airport according to the plan. She'd been a real pal about letting him use her car and not making him grovel for it, either. These past few days it had been great to have a car again. He'd filled up the gas tank this morning, which had pretty much tapped him out. But he'd accomplished a lot on Friday. Meeting face-to-face with manufacturers, brochure printers, suppliers and potential customers for his portable exercise equipment was more effective than e-mail and phone. He'd made some good deals and had a couple of new leads, but no money had come his way.

Well, payday from the pager store was tomorrow. Unfortunately, due to Christmas, he'd only worked twenty hours, but on the positive side, he'd already paid January's rent.

He pulled into Gwen's usual parking spot, which wasn't as close to her apartment as she was entitled. Some jerk who lived in the units across the back parked there. Alec had offered to challenge him, but Gwen wouldn't let him and said that the walk was good for her. In his opinion, Gwen could use a stiffer backbone, but that wasn't Alec's business.

He was only passing through.

Alec showered, changed into his last clean T-shirt— a giveaway from some charity 5K run three years ago—grabbed the pizza and beer, and headed for Gwen's apartment.

He'd already knocked when he replayed their last conversation in his head and suddenly realized how his cheap frozen pizza and single bottle of beer offering would look.

To stay in the running you've got to take her to clubs and restaurants and the bill runs up real quick.... Why didn't he just bang on the door and shout, "You're not worth it!"? It would be cheaper.

Maybe she wasn't home. But Gwen opened the door right then. "Hey, how's the car running?" She held out her hands for the keys.

If she hadn't been wearing her Scooby-Doo fuzzy slippers, he would have dropped the keys into her palm and taken his pizza with him. But...but he remembered the first time they'd met. He'd heard the Scooby-Doo theme music coming from inside her apartment and they'd discovered a mutual covert obsession with the cartoon character. He couldn't afford cable and she got the cartoon channel, so there had been a few instances when he'd watched episodes with her. Okay, more than a few.

"The car runs fine." He gave her the keys, then held up the plastic bags. "I brought pizza and beer. How about dinner?"

She blinked. "Is there a Scooby-Doo marathon on?"

It was his turn to blink. "Not that I know of. I thought it would be...be nice to..." *She thought he only wanted to eat with her so he could borrow her TV set.* Had he been that much of a moocher?

"To what?"

"You know, eat dinner together."

They stared at each other amid an unaccustomed awkwardness. What had he done? They'd eaten dinner together before, and yes, they usually ended up watching Gwen's TV. But this was different somehow. About the time Alec figured out it was because he'd never sought Gwen's company just for the sake of being with her, and why hadn't he, she pulled the pizza box out of the bag.

"You need a distraction while you eat this, huh?"

"Hey, that's the *premium* store brand," Alec shot back, relieved to fall into their usual pattern of mock insults and zingers.

"Ooo, the *premium* brand."

"Sarcasm? After I make a genuine spontaneous gesture of friendship and sharing—"

"All right, all right. I'll heat up the oven." Laughing, she took the pizza into the kitchen.

Back to normal. He exhaled and wandered over to

the sofa, noting her open laptop and the papers beside it. "Gwen?"

She looked at him through the kitchen bar.

"If you're busy—"

"Actually, you can help me. I'd like a man's opinion."

"Oh?" He held up one of the beers and she nodded. Twisting off the top, he set the bottle beside her laptop, careful to keep it away from the keyboard. He didn't mean to pry, but with the words Plan Of Attack written in eighteen-point type, he could hardly avoid reading. She'd made a column of words like "weakness, strength, objective, timeline, ammunition" and so forth. "What's up?"

"Just a minute."

He heard a buzz indicating that the oven had reached the baking temperature and then watched Gwen bend down to put the pizza in. Yeah, she was all right. Great female friend material. Twisting off the top of the second bottle, he took a swallow of beer and hoped again she wasn't too insulted by his pitiful offering.

He thought of her friend Lisa. No—Laurie. Whatever. *That* wasn't going anywhere. For a while there Linda—Laurie?—was sending all the right signals and under other circumstances...under other circumstances, Gwen wouldn't have been standing right beside them.

Why hadn't *she* ever looked at him like that?

Gwen threw away the pizza wrappings and came out of the kitchen. "This is really nice of you." Her smile was maybe a little too wide to be real.

Hell. "Look, Gwen, I know it's not much, especially after I—"

"You big doofus, you spent all your money, didn't you?"

Doofus? "Well, yeah."

She put a hand to her chest. "I'm *flattered*."

"Seriously? You are?"

"Yes. Now sit down and quit fussing."

"Fussing?" He never *fussed*. But he sat down.

Instead of being insulted, she was flattered. Women. He'd never understand them.

GWEN SAT beside him and handed him a brown foam insulator with the Kwik Koffee logo on it. Just when she'd given up on men, one of them had to go and do something sweet. Trying not to make a big deal out of Alec's gesture, Gwen nodded to her laptop screen as she fit her bottle into the foam rubber. "I'm going after a promotion," she said. "And I've been trying to think like a man."

"So you thought military instead of sports?"

"Yes." She hesitated. "I'm off sports."

"Works for me." He tilted back his head and swallowed, yet kept his eyes on her computer screen.

Gwen ruthlessly smothered a sigh and erased the mental image of Alec's jawline.

He tilted the bottle toward her list. "You haven't got very far."

"I know. That's where you come in. I'm currently on the staff of one of the regional directors. Kwik Koffee's got seven, but two of the largest regions need to be split and I think that'll be my best shot for a promotion.

Now, visualize the regional directors holed up in a fort under siege. I want in."

"I'm visualizing and I'm not seeing any women. Are there any women directors—is that the problem?"

"No women." Gwen shook her head. "But I think that's coincidence."

"Maybe. Maybe not."

"There are two assistant regional directors. Both women."

"And the fact that women are assistants is just coincidence?"

Gwen frowned. "I don't want to go there. The assistants are in the biggest regions, so logically, if the regions are split, they should get the promotion. I want you to tell me what an ambitious man would do in my position."

Alec sat back. "There's the time-honored, yet slimy, method of joining the same club and bonding in the steam room, a couple of rounds of golf a month, that kind of thing."

"I don't play golf."

"You should learn."

"I don't steam, either."

Alec laughed. "Put 'find something in common' on your list. Maybe the guy in charge collects wines or model trains. Or, I know—nothing beats a plate of warm brownies."

Only the wicked flash in his eye saved him.

"There is a *huge* difference between a plate of brownies and time in a steam room."

"That's a plate of *warm* brownies—okay!" he conceded when she opened her mouth. "But find out what he likes and give it to him."

Gwen raised her eyebrow.

He waved his beer bottle impatiently. "You know what I mean. Also, figure out who makes the promotion decisions. You have to make your boss look good to him."

"Why shouldn't I make myself look good to him?"

"You will be."

Gwen dutifully typed his suggestions. "I also know to analyze the work and find something that needs to be done, then volunteer to do it, but I can't figure out anything that needs to be done that I'm capable of doing. Kwik Koffee seems to run an efficient operation."

"Think small, but visible. Oh, yeah." Alec gestured for her to continue typing. "Think cost-cutting. Companies love it when you save money."

Gwen knew that, but she added it to the list to humor him. He was really getting into this corporate competitiveness.

"Reprice supplies or something. Then you can send a memo detailing what you found. Don't forget to print out your e-mail."

"Right, a paper trail." Gwen made a note to check prices on environmentally friendly coffee filters. They were a great idea, but had been too expensive in the past. Maybe the price had come down enough so that Kwik Koffee could reap the public relations benefit of a switch.

"Do you miss your job?" she asked as she typed. Alec had never gone into detail about his life before he came to live at Oak Villa Apartments, but Gwen got the impression that he'd been fairly high on the corporate ladder in a family-owned company.

He laughed. "I miss the salary! But this experience has forced me to look at life differently, which was no doubt what my granddad had in mind." He grimaced. "I suppose I'll have to admit it to him, too."

Gwen met his eyes. "Were you...fired?" she asked hesitantly.

"No! Hey, didn't I tell you about Granddad's big challenge?"

"You just told me you were trying to start your own business."

Alec took a deep breath and settled back on the sofa. It looked like it was going to be a long story. But that was okay. Gwen liked having Alec around. He wasn't any trouble. At least not much.

"Granddad came to this country with something like forty bucks in his pocket—I don't know, the amount is less every time he tells the story. But he started a little lunch-cart business, which grew and now we all work there. My dad and uncle really expanded the company. It was just strictly local and they worked their butts off taking it national." He stopped talking and looked off into the distance. Gwen had never seen him this somber before.

"Dad wasn't around much when I was little," he said, exhaling heavily.

"It must have been rough on your mother, too," Gwen said.

"I guess so." The way he said it told Gwen that he'd never considered his mother's point of view before. Well, he was now.

But apparently only for a second or two. "The thing that gets to me is that Granddad doesn't even acknowledge what his sons did or what any of us are doing. According to him, we're all just leeches benefiting from his hard work. And dad just…takes it. Drives me and my cousins nuts."

"So you quit?"

"Only temporarily. We want to develop the Web site and maybe open some stores in the malls, but Granddad won't listen to us, soooo…" Alec paused when the buzzer on the oven went off.

Gwen headed for the kitchen. "Keep talking. I can hear you."

"So we decided that one of us would start a business from the ground up under the same conditions—or as close as we could get—and prove to the old guy that we're not complete write-offs."

"And you lost?" She glanced through the bar as she got out plates.

Alec stared down at the beer in his hands, then looked up at her with a half smile. "No. I won."

Which was a pretty good insight into the male psyche, Gwen told herself. They liked challenges. Enjoyed them, even. She should start thinking that way about her promotion campaign.

"It's been tough, I won't kid you. I can't imagine how desperate and scared my grandfather must have been. At least I'm in the same country—the same city, even."

Gwen was cutting the pizza and trying to do so quietly so she could hear Alec, but managed to burn her thumb on hot cheese. She dropped the piece halfway between the plate and the cookie sheet and stuck her thumb in her mouth. Part of the topping was on the slice of pizza, the rest was on her counter. She nudged it into place, sort of, then looked up to find that Alec had left the sofa and was leaning his elbows on the bar as he watched her.

"Not much of a cook, are you?" He grinned.

"Like this never happened to you." She handed him the plate with the good pieces on it.

"Actually, no. Your mistake was in using plates. I just eat from the pan."

"Barbarian."

"Bad pizza cooker."

"*That's* the worst thing you can call me?" Gwen sat down and shoved her papers aside, then propped her Scooby-Doo slipper clad feet on the coffee table.

"My brain is running on low." Alec added his feet to the table, slouched down and propped the pizza plate on his stomach. His flat stomach. "I'll think of something after a few bites. In the meantime, speaking of Scooby-Doo—"

"Were we?"

"No, but we are now."

"Why?"

"Well, I've heard rumors of a New Year's Eve marathon." He gave her look out of the corner of his eye. "Got any party plans?"

Gwen's heart gave an extra thump. If only he'd stopped right then and there, but no, Alec continued.

"'Cause if you're going out, I wouldn't mind keeping an eye on your television for you." He grinned hopefully.

"I'm sure you wouldn't." Not, *hey Gwen, let's spend New Year's together* but *I want to watch cartoons on your TV.* Gwen took a moment to give herself a mental kick—she'd given up men. This was one of the reasons why.

"Won't charge you, either."

Oh no, not that smile, not the one he knew charmed women. She gave him a look to let him know *she* wasn't charmed. "Don't you have any plans? What about your friends? Have they abandoned you?"

Instantly, the smile faded and he looked down at his pizza. "They're all going to the Uptown Women's Center benefit 'gala.'" He used his fingers to make quote marks. "My girlfriend is on the steering committee. It's occupied her every waking moment since October."

Girlfriend? *Girlfriend?* Alec had a *girlfriend?* Not that it mattered to Gwen. It shouldn't matter to her. Wouldn't. Didn't.

"Have you noticed how nobody just throws a party for the sake of a good time anymore?" Alec was speaking rhetorically, which was a good thing since Gwen had frozen beside him. He hadn't noticed, which was also a good thing.

"It always has to benefit some organization. Why should we justify wanting to have a good time?"

"The Women's Center is a very worthy cause," Gwen managed. She also managed to sound tight-lipped. She wrapped her tight lips around the beer bottle and swallowed.

"Of course it is," Alec grumbled. "That's not the point here. The point is guilt-free partying."

"And so, what? You're boycotting?"

He mumbled something.

"What?" Gwen cupped her hand around her ear. "Is that a tiny tantrum I hear?"

"No." He shifted until his head was resting on the back of the sofa. "Stephanie—"

"That would be your girlfriend."

"Maybe, maybe not. Who knows anymore?"

"Well...this is just a thought...but if I spent hours and hours working on one of those charity things, I might be the teensiest bit put out if my boyfriend refused to go."

Still leaning against the sofa, he rolled his head to face her. "I can't afford to. My tux is back at my town house, along with my car, and I don't have the money to rent either. So no gala-going for me this New Year's."

"Wait a minute—you mean you own a car and you have a town—"

Alec held up a hand. "Technically, yes—"

"Is there any other way?"

"My grandfather didn't have a fancy place to live or his own—"

"It's *fancy*?"

"Well...it's...my cousin's wife is a decorator and she did the place for me, so it's okay."

"It's just *okay*."

"Okay, better than okay."

"Wood floors?"

"Yeah."

"Fireplace?"

"Yeah."

"Dining room?"

"I gotta eat someplace."

"Whirlpool tub?"

"Aren't those standard these days?"

"BMW or Mercedes?"

He gave her an exasperated look. "Beemer. Gwen, it doesn't matter. My grandfather wouldn't have had any of that stuff, so I can't either right now. That's why I traded places with the guy who used to live in the apartment here. Brad's living it up at my place, and I'm here with his damn cat." Apparently thoughts of the cat were worth two swallows of beer.

"I see." She crossed her arms and stared straight ahead. In her line of sight was a framed poster—Alec was no doubt used to original art—and put-it-together-yourself shelving displaying her Scooby-Doo memorabilia, which up to this point she'd thought was charmingly quirky. But now it looked kitschy and cheap.

"Gwen?" There was a hint of uncertainty in his voice, no doubt carefully calculated to elicit the most sympathy. "You understand about all that, don't you?"

"I'm feeling used," she declared. "Before, I felt used, but it was for a good cause."

"I'm still a good cause."

"You're a hopeless cause."

"And you're as bad as Stephanie."

Gwen bolted upright and gasped. "What a vile thing to say!"

Alec's lips quivered and then he started laughing.

She hadn't been serious, but he shouldn't have figured it out so quickly. Shaking her head, Gwen cleared away their plates. "At least that explains the cat. You have never struck me as a cat person."

"Armageddon is not a cat. Armageddon is demon spawn from hell."

"Poor kitty. With a name like Armageddon, what do you expect?"

"He earned the name. Thirty seconds at my place and he'd sprayed a white silk sofa."

Gwen rolled her eyes. "No real person has a white silk sofa."

"*I* do, or I do if the cleaners did their job. But Army came to the apartment with me that day and has avoided me ever since. He lives under the bed until I go into the bedroom. The rest of the time, he plots his escape."

Gwen rinsed their plates and put them in the dishwasher. "From what I remember, he's had a couple of successes."

"Yeah. Brad comes over and lures him back, though."

"The poor little thing."

"Don't feel sorry for Brad."

"I was talking about the cat and you know it. He just doesn't understand."

"He's not the only one," Alec muttered darkly.

Gwen returned to the sofa. "Is that an oblique reference to Stephanie and New Year's?"

He nodded.

"She doesn't quite see why you have to maintain the purity of the quest."

"Or words to that effect."

"I'll bet." Gwen stared at her Scooby-Doo slippers.

They stared back. "Your grandfather could have shopped at secondhand stores, right?"

"Oh, yeah. Wearing clothes from the church's charity box is always a featured part of the story. But if you think—"

"Buy your tux from Brad."

"What?"

"Offer him five or ten bucks for it. He's not going to be wearing it and you know it fits."

"That's..." Gwen could see the possibilities occur to Alec.

He gave her a slow, admiring smile. "That's brilliant."

"I thought so. And if you give me a ride over to my parents' house, then you can borrow my car." Sometimes she was too brilliant for her own good.

Alec kissed his fingers toward her. "Gwen, you are a prince among women."

"Is that anything like being a queen among men?"

He hesitated briefly, but tellingly. Very, very tellingly. "I didn't mean it to be." He laughed. If a forced chuckle could be called a laugh.

Gwen could attribute the hesitation to him being slow on the uptake, but Alec wasn't slow. No, for just a moment there, he'd considered the possibility that they were both sexually oriented in the same direction.

Was *this* what she was going to have to face? If a woman didn't want to be with a man, then...then... And just because she wasn't Alec's type didn't mean she wasn't *somebody's* type.

She'd show him. She'd...she'd go put on the skirt, that's what she'd do. Gwen jumped up. "Hey—I got a new skirt I was thinking of wearing on New Year's. How about a man's opinion?"

"Danger. Warning. Woman requesting clothing opinion. Alert, alert."

"Oh, stop." She headed for the bedroom. "I just want to know what you think."

"What I think is that nothing I say will be right," Alec called after her.

Gwen grabbed the skirt, hanger and all, and went back to her living room. She unsnapped the clamps, then held up the skirt. "I'll be with Laurie, so...you know." She hoped he'd fill in the blanks about at least holding her own beside Laurie.

And speaking of blanks—Alec stared at the skirt, then met her eyes. "It's...it's just a black skirt. It doesn't look all that short or tight."

"So you're saying that to appeal to a man, a skirt has to be short and tight?"

"Not...yes. Yes, it does."

She walked closer so he could see how the light made it shimmer, maybe even feel the fabric.

He was clearly unimpressed by shimmer. "Well, Gwen, it's a nice skirt."

Nice. Kiss of death.

"I don't know what you want me to say."

I want you to be overcome with lust, that's what. So much for the skirt's man-attracting potential.

"The sweatpants make it look lumpy. Why don't you put it on?"

"All right, I will."

Gwen returned to the bedroom, suspecting that the reason she hadn't put the skirt on in the first place was because if Alec *was* overcome with lust, she'd forget that she'd given up men and men like Alec were exactly the reason why. He'd talked about Laurie being high-maintenance, but if he took off his shirt—a pleasant, but distracting prospect—he'd have "high-maintenance" tattooed across his chest.

Already, she'd offered him her car and helped him with his love life—a love life that didn't include her. Now, she was putting on the skirt after she swore she wouldn't just so he'd find her attractive. And she'd just cooked dinner for him. Hadn't she?

Gwen stepped into the skirt, thinking that she probably ought to put on panty hose, and pulled it up. Pulled...now more of an easing...sucked in her stomach...more...gave up on fastening the hook until after the zipper was zipped...zipped two inches and...

And staring in horror as her white, pizza-filled belly remained exposed because her hips and thighs had taken up all the room in the skirt.

3

SAVED. SAVED FROM herself. Putting on the skirt to attract Alec—what had she been thinking? Or rather, why had she been thinking it?

Fortunately, when she returned, he was typing some manly strategy he'd thought of into her laptop, and didn't seem to remember the skirt.

Not fitting into the skirt didn't matter. And yet Gwen ate salad with dressing on the side and avoided ice cream until Wednesday. She wasn't dieting—she just suddenly developed a real fondness for naked lettuce. Besides, her ice cream day was Friday. Okay, Thursday through Saturday—Wednesday, if it had been a really rough week. But never Monday or Tuesday. Never. Oh, maybe a bite or two from Friday's pint—but that was absolutely *it*.

And did the skirt care about naked lettuce or avoiding ice cream? Did it cooperate by at least letting Gwen zip the zipper completely? No.

So when New Year's Eve rolled around, Gwen had to resort to her "safe" outfit—black silky pants, elastic waist, and the cute, but scratchy, Lurex sweater with the gold and silver champagne glasses all over it. Some of the glasses had bubbles coming out of them and Gwen had to stand up straight or a couple of the bubbles would be positioned suggestively.

The sweater had a V-neck and by aggressively pull-ing it down and standing with her arms just so, Gwen summoned up more cleavage than she had last year.

At least not all the extra pounds had gone to her hips.

She released the hem of the sweater and the neckline sprang back into mother-approved territory.

Gwen sighed and spent more time on her makeup. Why, she didn't know. She hadn't been kidding when she'd told Laurie that the pickings were slim among her parents' New Year's Eve crowd.

As the thought occurred to her, Alec knocked on her door. She knew it was Alec because he was the only one knocking on her door these days. And she sud-denly knew why she was wrestling with lip liner.

Alec came from a background where the women wore lip liner. They didn't just buy it with good inten-tions, then leave it in their bathroom drawers until it dried out and crumbled when they got around to using it on New Year's Eve to impress him.

Not that she was trying to impress him. He knocked again. Gwen threw down the lip liner, slashed at her mouth with lipstick and hurried to the door, then slowed when she realized he wasn't going anywhere—she had the car keys, after all.

Speaking of...where had she put her purse? Right, back in the bedroom so she could exchange her leather carryall for a petite evening bag that was basically use-less. She was just going to her mother's, but Alec would see her and Gwen had *some* pride, misplaced though it was.

He knocked again.

"All right! I heard you the first time you banged on the door!" He must be eager to see Stephanie.

Irritated, Gwen flung open the door. "You're just going to have to wait until I get my purse and a jack—"

Hands shoved in his pockets, Alec lounged against the iron railing at the top of the stairs outside her door. He looked...he looked...well, certainly worthy of lip liner.

He'd done the slicked-back thing with his hair, only on him it looked good. And the tux was...was black and shawl-collared with a shirt so white it hurt to look at it. He wore the traditional black bow tie and his shirt studs had to be a studly onyx and not plastic.

Gwen hung on to the doorknob with a death grip and tried to remember what she'd been saying. It would help if he'd give her a clue, but Alec wasn't even looking at her. No, judging by the direction of his gaze, he was looking at her...bubbles.

"Nice sweater." Grinning, Alec raised his eyes to hers. "Very...effervescent."

"Ha ha." Gwen straightened. "You have cat hair on your tux."

"Damn cat." He spoke with resignation and brushed at his arms.

"Pant leg," Gwen pointed. "Come in and I'll get you some masking tape."

"Why?" He followed her in and shut the door.

Gwen ignored her wobbly legs and took off for the kitchen. "For the cat hair."

She rummaged around in her kitchen drawer and brought him the roll of tape. "Wrap it around your hand sticky side out."

"Wouldn't it make sense to invest in a lint brush?"

"I have a lint brush, but I don't want cat hair in it."

Alec smiled in a worldly amused way and wrapped his hand in the tape.

It was so not fair. He looked fabulous and she could only aspire to cute with slightly risqué bubbles. And then only if she slouched.

While Alec removed all traces of Armageddon, Gwen went back to the bedroom, packed the tiny purse and found her trench coat. It was khaki and didn't go with her outfit. Why was she only thinking of that *now*? On the other hand, was it really cold enough for a jacket? What had she worn last year? Probably the trench coat.

Her car had a heater. She'd just ditch the coat.

Then she remembered that she needed an overnight bag which would *really* spoil her look, but she no longer cared. If she took too much more time, then Alec would come looking for her and the thought of Alec in her bedroom... She refused to entertain thoughts of Alec in her bedroom.

Alec was still in her kitchen disposing of the make-shift lint brush in the trash can under the sink. "So how do I look? Any more cat hair?" He held out his arms and turned around.

Gwen stuck her nose in the air. "Absolutely fab, dahling. Seriously, you look great—like you're wearing Armani."

A beat went by. Something about the expression on his face...Gwen cringed inwardly. "You *are* wearing Armani, aren't you?"

"I got a great deal." Alec took her overnight satchel

from her. "I paid fifteen bucks for it yesterday afternoon. Got it from a guy who found it hanging in the back of his closet." He held open the door for her.

"What luck." Without meeting his eyes, Gwen waited until he was outside, locked the door and handed him the keys.

Alec stood staring at them as they lay in his palm reflecting the multicolored blinking from her neighbor's Christmas lights.

Maybe she should have taken the Scooby-Doo in a Santa hat off the key ring. Gwen wondered if Stephanie liked Scooby-Doo. "Sorry, my Rolls is in the shop. It needed an oil change."

He didn't even crack a smile. "I appreciate this, Gwen." Gesturing for her to precede him down the stairs, he muttered something that sounded like, "I hope Stephanie does," but Gwen couldn't be sure.

Alec was in a strange mood. As he drove her to her parents' house, he smiled and joked back at her, but there wasn't any zing to it.

Gwen was fascinated to realize that a good-looking Alec without zing wasn't nearly as attractive as a rumpled Alec using charm to mooch from her, even though they both knew what he was doing.

Well, wasn't this a fun way to start New Year's Eve?

"I'll be spending the night at my folks'," she reminded him when the conversation lagged, "so just come get me sometime tomorrow afternoon."

"Okay."

"If you call first, I'll be ready and you can make the trip during the halftime of some game."

"Okay."

"Or, you could just show up if it's more convenient."

"Gee, Gwen, roll over and I might scratch your tummy."

Jerk. "Try it, and I'll bite off your fingers while I'm peeing on your carpet."

He laughed. Finally. But he was still a jerk.

"Sorry. I was being a jerk."

"I was just thinking that."

"Ignore me."

She'd like to, but he wasn't very ignorable. "What's wrong?" *Stop there. Right there. No! Don't—* "Wasn't Stephanie glad to hear that you're going to be there tonight after all?" *Slit your wrists. Now. There's a nail file in the glove compartment.*

"Yes." He added nothing else.

Fine, then. Her attempt at filler conversation had gone nowhere, so she'd just let him brood.

During the ensuing silence, she mentally chanted *his happiness is not my responsibility.* The last time she'd chanted that was in connection with Eric.

The situation with Alec was completely different, yet here she was, catering to him in the same way. Why did she keep doing this to herself? She'd recognized her problem with men, so why couldn't she avoid making it so easy for them to take advantage of her? She didn't want to spend all day at her parents' house, yet she'd practically begged Alec to keep the car as long as he wanted.

It was her old pattern with men—always putting herself and what she wanted second. Taking care of them, inconveniencing herself and in essence training them not to consider her wants at all. She frequently caught herself doing it at work, too. Not good.

It was apparently going to take more than giving up men to break the habit.

They were winding their way along Memorial Drive nearing the area where her parents lived. Gwen indicated where Alec should turn. "I'd appreciate it if you could get me by noon tomorrow. Any later and Mom will feel that she has to make a production out of lunch and I know she'll be tired after the party."

"Will do."

That wasn't so hard, was it? Gwen felt the beginnings of empowerment. "Turn down the next street and go all the way to the end."

"The house with all the floodlights?"

"That's the one."

He pulled into the driveway behind the catering van. "Looks like your parents' party is a major deal."

"It is. Tons of people in and out all night." She reached for the door handle and was touched to see that Alec got out, retrieved her satchel for her and carried it all the way to the front door.

"Again, I appreciate this."

His voice was warmly sincere and just for a second, Gwen wanted to drag him inside like some trophy and display him to her parents. Instead, she reached for her bag. "No prob. See you tomorrow."

Alec shoved his hands into his pockets and tilted his head to one side. "Gwen?"

She'd already pushed open the door. "Yes?"

"You do look good." He delivered the line just matter-of-factly enough so she knew he was serious.

She stared at him as her heart thumped wildly. *Say something witty.* "Thanks." So much for wit.

He nodded once and headed back to the car, passing Laurie who'd emerged from one of the parked cars.

"Hi—Laurie, is it?"

Looking thunderstruck, Laurie managed an, "Uh-huh."

Alec lifted a hand. "Happy New Year."

Laurie turned and watched him until he got into Gwen's car, then joined Gwen on the porch.

"That was your *neighbor?*" Laurie was wearing something tight and shiny.

"Yeah. Cleans up real nice for a mechanic, doesn't he?"

"Well, *yeah.*" She followed Gwen inside. "How come you just let him drive off like that?"

"He's going to some benefit."

"And he can't come in and be sociable for ten minutes?" Laurie stopped in front of the mirror in the foyer and checked her perfect appearance.

Gwen tugged at her sweater. "He's got a girlfriend."

"I repeat, he couldn't come in—"

"Drop it, Laurie."

"But...wait a minute, you aren't wearing the skirt!"

Sighing, Gwen headed for the spare bedroom to stow her satchel. "You are expecting *way* too much from my parents' party."

"I was thinking of your neighbor."

"You're expecting way too much from Alec, too."

Laurie gave her an arch look. "Have you worn the skirt in front of him?"

"No." Gwen wanted to avoid talking about the skirt. "Come on. Let's go make friends with the bartender."

She and Laurie heard voices as they approached the living room. And then they walked into chaos.

"ALEC! YOU'RE HERE." Stephanie gripped his arm and gave him an air kiss.

"How are things going, Steph?" He'd found her rearranging items in the silent auction display.

She turned to look around the hotel ballroom at the sea of silver and navy blue tables. Her hair was all glued to the top of her head, aside from a couple of curls that brushed her shoulders and drew attention to her neck. Nice.

Except he caught himself thinking of a certain sweater with stray bubbles that made him smile.

"We're sold out," she whispered. "I'm so nervous!"

"What's there to be nervous about?" The band had shown up and was doing a sound check and white-coated bartenders lounged at their stations, so the two main criteria for a good party had been satisfied. Everything looked well under control to Alec.

"A million things could go wrong!" Steph drew a deep breath, nicely filling her strapless silver dress.

Alec was reminded that he hadn't seen Steph for several weeks. He drew her to him, tweaking a blond curl. "That means a million things could go right." He bent to kiss her, but Steph pulled back.

"Alec, not now!"

"Then, when?" he murmured, ignoring the unexpected twinge of relief.

"Is that all you can think about?"

"With you in that dress...yes." It was a canned response, something to ease her nerves.

Stephanie gazed steadily at him. "You drop out of sight for months and think you can just pick up where we left off?"

He straightened and gazed down at her. "*Zoinks.*" It was a Scooby-Doo reference. Gwen would have caught it.

But he underestimated Stephanie. "Oh, grow up." She faced him, but as she spoke her eyes constantly scanned the arriving crowd.

"I am growing up. I'm taking life much more seriously these days. Poverty will do that to you."

"You're playing the prince and the pauper and watching cartoons." Stephanie adjusted the bow on a spa basket and straightened the bidding sheet, placing a small silver pencil at the top. Then she moved on to the next item and checked it off her list.

"I thought you understood what I'm trying to accomplish."

"I understand that you announced that you were going to start your own business the way your grandfather had. I even understand that you want the same handicaps that he had. And I understand that you like the challenge." She checked off another item—this one for two round-trip tickets to Paris and a week in a hotel—before turning to him. "What I do not understand is why you didn't discuss it with me first."

Because he would have accepted the challenge no matter what her opinion. Alec had enough sense of self-preservation to avoid telling Stephanie that, especially right now. She was admittedly nervous. He'd cut her some slack.

But as she continued talking, he realized this was more than a case of nerves. Steph was dealing with a whole lot of repressed anger. "You knew how happy I was to be asked to be on this steering committee. It means the board trusts me not to let the Center down. This is their only fund-raiser. How well we do tonight determines how many women and children we can help next year. And it's never enough. *Never*."

"Steph...everything looks great. You'll do fine."

Her jaw hardened and tension visibly marred her lovely neck. "I want more than fine—I want fabulous. I want record-breaking. And I wanted your support. But just when things were gearing up, you dropped out of sight. I've had to do everything—make donation calls, go to all the progress meetings, even attend the donor cocktail party this evening—by myself. You didn't get *one* lousy donation for the silent auction. Not even from your own company! Don't think that the absence of Fleming Snack Foods has gone unnoticed. I'm so embarrassed."

She had a right to be. "I'm sorry." And he was. "Granddad will make a contribution—he always does. You should have reminded me."

Stephanie pierced him with a look. "I shouldn't have had to."

"No, you shouldn't have, but Steph, I've been working my tail off."

"Oh, yes. Your strenuous minimum-wage job at the pager store."

Alec's guilt faded. He hadn't volunteered to work on

the benefit tonight, though he was willing to acknowledge that if he hadn't accepted his grandfather's challenge, he would have helped her. "There's a lot more going on in my life than my survival job, which you'd know if you'd bothered to come and see me."

"I did, if you'll recall."

He did. They'd sat around and talked, but the conversation never caught fire. She'd brought him up to speed on all the news of their friends, some of which they'd already discussed on the telephone, but there didn't seem to be anything else to talk about.

In the end, sniffling, Stephanie claimed the cat dander was bothering her and they'd called it a night. It was the first time Alec had harbored positive feelings toward Armageddon.

"Okay, you came over once," he conceded. "But after that, you never came again. You never asked about my progress and you never showed any interest in what I was doing."

"Because, Alec, it was apparent that you didn't want me to be a part of what you're doing. You made a huge life decision without giving me a thought."

It was true. He hadn't considered their relationship that significant. Obviously she had.

"And as for showing interest…did you even *once* ask about any of this?" She waved her arm around the room. "Did *you* come and visit *me*? We could have gone to dinner or met some friends for drinks. But no."

"I don't have a car and I couldn't afford to take you to all the places we used to go," he ground out.

"Oh, that's right. Your pseudo poverty."

She could have footed the bill for an evening out,

Alec thought. Had she ever? "It's sounding to me like you're only interested in me when I can afford to spend money on you."

"I don't like what you're implying."

Alec thought he'd been pretty clear, but he'd drop the subject for now. "Hey. We shouldn't have let so much time go by without seeing each other. The phone's not the same. Now that you're almost finished with the party tonight, plan to come hang out with me next week."

Stephanie stopped fiddling with a display of wine bottles and looked at him, her beautiful blue eyes unblinking. "And do what?"

Alec shoved his hand into his pocket and encountered Gwen's keys. His fingers found the Scooby-Doo charm and he felt the corner of his mouth lift. "Talk. Just be together."

Stephanie's cool gaze warmed and she took a step toward him. He could smell her perfume. It wasn't his favorite, it was something new. Heavier. "Talk about what?" She brushed at his lapel, maybe removing a stray cat hair, maybe only finding an excuse to stand closer. "About us?"

Us. Was there an "us"?

She was gorgeous and she knew it—hc'd told her so, too. He had no problem with gorgeous. He liked gorgeous.

His fingers closed over the key ring until the edges pressed painfully against his knuckles. He also liked smart and funny and comfortable and gabby.

Stephanie was smart and she could talk. She might be on the serious side, but she always laughed at jokes and was great in a group. She got along with his friends and he was okay with hers. But comfortable? No. Stephanie was not comfortable.

Just how important was comfort to him, anyway?

"Stephanie? Oh, hon, everything looks *gorgeous!*"

Stephanie brightened when mutual friends, accompanied by a man who was maybe a decade older than Alec, approached.

The man gave her an admiring look, maybe just a bit more admiring than Alec, as her boyfriend-of-record, should permit to go unchallenged.

But he didn't challenge the guy, didn't walk over and wrap an arm around her waist, because he didn't feel like it. He felt...nothing, actually. Whatever buttons Stephanie had once pushed had been disconnected.

And he had a pretty good idea who'd disconnected them.

4

"I AIN'T MOVING the pie-anny until Miz Kempner done tell me to."

"Cut the cornpone accent, Troy." The caterer, Katherine Yancy, decked out in full chef's toque, was going nose to nose with the head bartender.

As Gwen and Laurie stepped into the living room, Katherine turned to a tuxedo-clad man who sat at the black Baldwin grand piano. "Lenny? Please move the piano."

"Can't. Union rules." He played a rippling arpeggio. "I'm the talent."

"Glad you told me. I wouldn't have known," Katherine snapped.

Three bar stations were all jammed next to each other. Behind Katherine stood an army of servers with nothing to serve.

"Well, Happy New Year." Laurie approached one of the bars.

"What's going on?" Gwen didn't intend to speak as loudly as she did.

Everyone heard her. Everyone began talking at once.

"Hey!" Gwen waved them quiet. "Where're my parents?"

Everyone looked at everyone else. Katherine spoke. "Your mother is in the bedroom. She won't come out."

Only a disaster would have kept her mother from directing party preparations. Fortunately, Gwen knew the drill from countless entertainments past.

"Katherine, you've been with us before. Do you remember last year's setup?"

"The grand buffet table goes there." She pointed to the piano and glared at Lenny, who responded by playing the wicked witch theme from *The Wizard of Oz.*

"Right." Gwen approached the head bartender. "I'm Gwen Kempner. Your name is Troy?"

"Yes, ma'am." He'd dropped the accent, she noticed.

"Troy, one of those bar stations should be upstairs in the game room on the wall opposite the pool table. The other can stay right there and put the third in the foyer."

He nodded to his staff and Gwen faced the piano. "Laurie, help me move this."

"*Move* the pi—"

"Laurie."

"I was just going to ask where we were moving it."

Gwen jerked her head to the side as Laurie approached the piano and placed her palms against the front edge so she wouldn't damage her nails. She bent forward arching her back. Judging by the expression of one of the bartenders, the view from the front must have been spectacular. "It's heavy," she said breathily.

Fat lot of help *she* was going to be. "That's because it's a piano," Gwen said through gritted teeth. Didn't Laurie see that they were in the middle of a crisis? "We're going to turn it around so the keyboard is against the window." Gwen braced herself against the curved side. Katherine and the bartender who'd noticed Laurie joined them.

"Hey!" Lenny stood and slithered from behind the keyboard. "I want my right side toward the room."

"Lenny, you aren't moving the piano, so you don't get a say in where it goes." Gwen pushed. If Lenny had joined them, she would have let him have the more visible position he wanted, even though it would have crowded the buffet. But he remained faithful to the union rules so she twirled the piano one hundred eighty degrees.

"Thanks," Gwen told her helpers, but Katherine was already gesturing for her staff to set up in the space where the piano had been.

And Laurie was clearly expressing gratitude to the good-looking bartender who'd helped them.

Fine. Gwen carried the bench over to the keyboard and gestured. Lenny sullenly seated himself and began leafing through his music. He'd probably express his displeasure by playing a long medley of mediocre hits from the seventies. He might even sing.

But Gwen had other things to worry about besides a pouting Lenny and Laurie distracting the bar staff. She checked her watch. It was a little past seven-thirty, which meant that early arrivals and party hoppers could be there at any time.

Hurrying down the hall, she knocked on her parents' bedroom door, interrupting a low, but intense argument.

"Go away!" her mother called.

"Mom, it's Gwen. Let me in." She tried the knob, but the door was locked.

"Gwen, your father and I are having a discussion. Please leave."

"Suzanne, there's nothing to discuss!" she heard her father declare.

A second later, the door opened and he pushed past her. Gwen slipped inside before her mother could stop her.

Suitcases and clothing littered her parents' normally neat room. Not a good omen. "Mom?"

Still in her robe, Gwen's mother sat on the edge of the bed. There were signs that she'd been crying, but now she looked more angry than anything else.

"He can't do this to me."

Gwen didn't need to ask who. "Do what?"

"*This!*" Suzanne jerked her arm outward, indicating the suitcases and the pile of suits decorated with garlands of ties.

"Is Dad...leaving you?"

"Yes—"

Gwen gasped.

"Not that kind of leaving." Her mother stood. "He's quit his job and is going off to find himself. As usual, he has not bothered to ask directions."

"Dad quit his job?" Gwen sank onto the spot her mother had vacated.

Suzanne stepped over the debris and headed to the bathroom where she turned on her makeup lights and studied her reflection.

"That's what he said. He made the announcement just after the caterers arrived." She opened a jar and began removing the trails of melted mascara on her cheeks. "He felt that I'd have so much to do, I wouldn't have time to make a big deal out of it."

"I guess you showed him, huh?"

Her mother gazed at her for a long moment, then went back to repairing her makeup. "I am well aware that you disapprove of the way I've chosen to live my life."

"That's because you haven't lived your life, you've lived *Dad's* life." And now look what's happened, Gwen thought, but decided not to say.

"We have a partnership, though I don't expect you to understand. An *equal* partnership." She sniffed. "At least that's what I always thought, but Tom seems to have forgotten that I've worked just as hard for his position as he has. And now...now he thinks he can just throw it all away without a word to me. Well, he can't. I won't let him."

"Mom—"

"Gwen, would you please do something with the clothes and suitcases? Just stuff everything out of sight and we'll sort it out later."

Gwen took her mother at her word and began shoving the suitcases back into the closet and tossing the piles of clothes on top.

"Gwen," came her mother's voice. "Go find your father and tell him to get dressed."

Gwen dumped the last of the suits and shut the closet door before they slithered down the clothes mountain she'd made.

Her father might be having a midlife crisis, but now was not the time to argue or analyze. Now was the time for damage control.

Gwen might not agree with her mother's choice to spend her life as the perfect corporate wife, but that didn't mean she wasn't going to do everything she could to help her now. She knew how important the annual New Year's Eve party was. Most of the guests were business associates, just as at all her parents' entertainments. Being treated to a marital spat would damage the careful image her parents presented to the world.

Gwen found her father in the garage. He was dressed in full camouflage—creased camo, as though he'd put on the clothes right out of the bags. Like those opened plastic bags littering the floor by a generator she'd never seen before.

Gwen took a moment to readjust her mental image of her father. Surrounding him and piled on top of a brand-new black SUV, was camping equipment. She could see price tags on most of it. "Hey, Dad. What did you do, rob a Boy Scout?"

"Hello, Gwen," he said somberly. "You'll be taking your mother's side in this, I assume."

Her heart sank. "Are there sides?"

Her father slowly withdrew a wicked looking Toledo steel hunting knife from a leather holder. "There is the side of the status quo and there is the side of slowing down. Simplifying." The blade flashed in the light of a Coleman lantern.

"Since when did it take so much junk to simplify?"

"It's all I need to survive in this world, Gwen." Her father put the knife in a Day-Glo orange backpack.

Oh, boy. "Are you going on one of those corporate-

survival-bonding-in-the-wilderness kind of things?"
Please say yes.

"No."

"Hunting with your buds?" She didn't think her father hunted, though he'd been on a deep-sea fishing trip or two.

"No." Her father continued his methodical packing. He opened package after package, discarded the wrappings by simply dropping them on the floor, and putting the batteries, matches, fuel canisters and the like into his backpack.

"What are you doing, Dad?" Gwen knew she sounded irritated, and she was—more because she'd had to ask him than because he was exhibiting symptoms of a survivalist fanatic.

"I've retired."

"Fr-from your job?" Her father was only in his mid-fifties and he'd never seemed the retiring sort. Gwen gasped as a thought occurred to her. "Were you laid off?"

"No!" It was the only emotion he'd expressed so far. He drew a breath as though to deliberately calm himself. "I've bought a cabin on the Northwest Pacific coast and I'm going to live there."

"By yourself?"

"Apparently so."

"Did you even ask Mom?"

"Your mother refuses to consider it."

Actually, the Seattle area was a great place and really popular right now. A vacation home in that area might be something her mother would like. "Well, Dad, did you tell her what kind of place it was? Like, how many bedrooms, baths, what's nearby—"

"Nothing is nearby. That's the point. This is a single-room cabin with a woodburning stove and a marvelous stone fireplace. Outside is clear, cool, honest well water." He opened another package of batteries and put them in a flashlight, the third one Gwen had seen.

"Are you saying there's no electricity?"

He turned the flashlight on and off, then packed it away. "It isn't necessary."

Yeah, right. "Dad...Mom doesn't even like to stay in hotels without room service. No wonder she won't spend her vacation there."

"As I said, I'm going there to live. I leave tomorrow morning. A new year, a new life." His smile didn't seem like the smile of a crazy man.

Gwen felt completely helpless and ineffective. "What about the party?" she asked simply because she couldn't think of anything else to say.

Her father, still wearing his newly gentle smile, reached out and squeezed her shoulder. "Go help your mother."

Nodding numbly, Gwen slipped back into the house.

She stood in the doorway of the living room and heard Lenny fooling around with a version of "Raindrops Keep Falling on My Head," saw Katherine giving the buffet table last-minute garnishes, noticed that Laurie was behind the main bar with the handsome bartender and saw another bartender in the entryway holding glasses above a bucket of ice until they fogged, then wiping them.

She did not see her mother.

Okay. She knew what to do next. Striding over to the foyer bar, she said, "Scotch on the rocks" and knocked the drink back before her tongue could register the assault.

Scotch was a man's drink and Gwen was trying to accustom herself to it. Or burn her esophagus, one of the two.

She blinked rapidly, hoping to evaporate the tears before they spilled over onto her cheeks and also hoping the bartender hadn't noticed.

A cloud of perfume announced her mother's arrival. "Where's Tom?" she asked as she swept by Gwen on her way to the door.

"Dad's still in the garage."

"And the Brillsteins are here already. I saw Sophie's new Jag drive up." Her mother's jaw tightened, then she put on her party face just as the doorbell sounded.

Through her tears, Gwen watched her mother straighten her shoulders, then throw open the door with a sweeping gesture. "Charles! Sophie! Happy New Year!"

"LAURIE, please don't leave me!" Gwen grasped her friend's arm as Laurie primped in the bedroom mirror. "At least not for a bartender."

"Gwen, honey. If it makes you feel any better, Brian isn't really a bartender. He was just filling in for his little brother. He's actually an assistant D.A." She peeled Gwen's fingers off her upper arm and grabbed her purse and jacket. "We invented three new drinks tonight." She sighed. "He named one after me."

"Gee, I can't possibly compete with an alcoholic drink."

Laurie smiled at her. "You sure can't."

Gwen wouldn't mind an alcoholic drink right about now. It had been over three hours since the scotch. Three hours of watching her mother flit around, pretending Gwen's father wasn't periodically tromping through the living room in his camo gear, announcing his retirement and showing people the equipment in the garage and pictures of the cabin.

Every time Suzanne referred to the cabin as a vacation getaway, Tom corrected her gently, but insistently.

Matters weren't helped by Tom burning bridges as he told business associates his true opinions of them and the way they'd done business for the past twenty-five years. These opinions were never complimentary, but were always stated in an eerily pleasant, calm, matter-of-fact voice that led people to believe he was joking. Then her father would elaborate to show that no, he wasn't joking. Her mother would then utter shrill inanities accompanied by loud trills of laughter in a futile attempt to drown him out. As a result, by eleven-thirty, the carnage was complete. Guests had fled, apparently warning new arrivals off as well.

Gwen could hardly blame Laurie for wanting to leave. She followed her out of the bedroom. Brian, the bartender, was waiting by the front door, silently watching as Gwen's mother ripped one of the cabin pictures into tiny pieces and threw them into the air.

"Happy New Year!" she snarled, and retreated to the bedroom.

"Is it midnight already?" Tom asked the room at

large. "We should make a toast. Bartender, champagne for everyone!"

"Hey, are you going to be all right?" Brian asked Gwen as Laurie slipped her arm around his waist. "We can stay...or Laurie can stay." He looked down at her. "If you do, I *will* call. I mean it."

Brian was just dripping sincerity—or testosterone. Probably both. It figured that Laurie would find one of the good guys.

"No, no." Gwen shooed them away. "Go on. *I* don't even want to stay."

"Are you sure?" Laurie asked unenthusiastically, but apparently convincingly enough for Brian, who rewarded her with a squeeze around her waist.

"Yeah." Gwen opened the door. "Happy New Year."

"Oh, it is." They both grinned at each other sickeningly.

As they swayed toward one another, Gwen shut the door so she wouldn't see the inevitable kiss.

Sure she'd temporarily given up men, but she didn't need a visual reminder of all the lovely benefits she'd given up with them.

Yes, it was a very good thing that she'd temporarily—and it was only temporary until she had time for them again—given up men, or she'd really regret wrapping Alec up in a great big bow and sending him off to his girlfriend. A girlfriend she hadn't even known existed. But that wasn't her business and it didn't matter *at all* that he was off making someone named Stephanie deliriously happy instead of...

instead of watching the New Year's Eve Scooby-Doo marathon with Gwen. Nope. No regrets for her.

Slowly, she walked into the living room, watching as her father poured champagne for the staff.

Lenny, eyes closed, was emoting Neil Diamond.

Katherine poked her head into the room and gestured to her. As Gwen made her way across the room, her father accosted her.

"Champagne?"

She spread her hands. "I don't have a glass."

"Here then." He handed her the bottle.

And Gwen took it, drank a swig, and handed it back. It was that kind of night.

Katherine was frowning at the kitchen door. "There are a lot of leftovers," she murmured.

"Package them up and put them in the refrigerator," Gwen told her. The party was over. A lot of things were probably over.

"I have been. The refrigerator and the freezer out in the garage are full."

"Did you invite the staff to have something to eat?"

"Oh, yes." Katherine avoided her eyes.

Gwen spied one of the expensive spiral-sliced hams still unopened.

And she thought of Alec. They'd be eating leftovers for a week. No, she shouldn't be finding excuses to see Alec. But she couldn't let the ham go to waste, could she? "Just package up the rest and I'll take it home with me."

Because Gwen was *not* going to spend the night in this house. Whatever was going on with her father was between her parents. Gwen's place was eating leftovers in front of her television set. Her father had a new car—she'd borrow the old one and drive herself home.

In the distance, she heard the doorbell. Oh, great.

Katherine heard it, too, and professional that she was, she waved for two of her staff to check the food out front.

Neither Gwen's mother nor her father appeared in the living room, and Gwen decided not to alert them. She'd just make up some story and send away whoever was at the door. She snagged a bottle of unopened champagne as she passed the foyer bar, intending to give it to the newcomers as a consolation prize.

Drawing a deep breath, she opened the door. "Hap—Alec!"

Hands shoved in his pockets, Alec looked at her quizzically from the doorway. "I thought I had the wrong house." He indicated the empty street. "What happened to the party?"

"Oh, Alec, I'm *so* glad you're here." Gwen yanked him inside the house and thrust the bottle of champagne at him.

"Just a minute..." He cocked his head, then looked sternly at her. "Is that 'Muskrat Love'?"

Gwen whimpered and brought her hands to her temples.

"There, there." He drew her in his arms and patted her back. "Alec will make it all better. Hey, you. Piano guy. No tips for Captain and Tennille!"

The music immediately changed to *Auld Lang Syne*.

In spite of the horror of the evening, Gwen chuckled,

and stepped back, liking how it felt to be held by him just a little too much. Make that a lot too much.

"If you don't mind me saying so, I think I've solved the party's problem."

"Ha." Gesturing for Alec to follow her, Gwen led the way to the kitchen, babbling the entire story.

She continued to babble while they loaded boxes and sacks of leftovers into her trunk. Alec showed the great, good sense to keep quiet and let her talk. After they'd been in the car for a few minutes, Gwen wound down and realized that Alec had gone way beyond being a good listener. He was, for all purposes, mute.

Gwen drew a shuddering breath and leaned her head back, grateful that Alec was driving. Grateful that he'd showed up just as she'd reached her limit...why *had* he been at her parents' house, anyway?

She sat up and tried to read her watch by the streetlights they passed.

"It's not midnight, yet," he said into the silence.

"No, it's not." Gwen turned so she could study him. He kept his eyes fixed on the road.

"It's not midnight yet," Gwen reiterated. "What are you doing here?"

"I'm rescuing you."

"And I'm very grateful, but how did you know I needed rescuing?"

"I don't know...some recessive white knight gene?"

"Cute. Now what happened to *your* party?" *And where's Stephanie?*

"We finished early and—"

"On New Year's Eve?"

He slid a quick glance at her. "*You* finished early."

"We were finished before we started."

"I hear that." He exhaled heavily. "Let's just say that my evening was on par with yours. Had better music, though."

After several more minutes of silence went by, Gwen said, "I am aware that you don't want to discuss it. Are you aware that I'm going to badger you until I get the whole story, or enough of the story to satisfy my curiosity—*which* I feel entitled to having invested in this evening?"

"I'm aware of that. Are *you* aware that I could have just come by for you tomorrow as planned and you'd be none the wiser?"

"I'm not wiser *now*."

She could see his jaw work and figured he was clamping his back teeth together. She sighed. "Okay. Fine. Don't tell me."

"Gwen—"

"Shh. I've changed my mind."

"It's just that—"

She held up a hand. "I don't want to hear it."

Not that she expected reverse psychology to work on Alec. She *did* realize belatedly that pressuring him revealed an interest in his affairs—poor word choice—that she would rather he didn't notice.

"Gwen—"

"Do you realize that I have an *entire* cooked ham as well as a smoked turkey breast in my trunk?"

Grinning, he slid an arm along the back of the car seat. "Do *you* realize I'd rather see in the New Year with you than anyone else?"

5

IT WAS TRUE. Right now, Alec wanted to be with Gwen more than anyone else he knew.

He'd suspected he'd made the wrong choice for his evening when Stephanie had thrown him a startled look after he let the Paris trip for two go without bidding on it during the auction. His next clue was when he'd noticed that their table was set for nine and all the others were set for eight. And he'd strongly suspected it after the dancing, when they'd sat down to a dinner of tiny food with fancy sauces and Stephanie called the wine captain over so Alec could buy champagne for the table. But he'd truly realized he'd rather be with Gwen when Steph exchanged a look with Robert Vanderhof, sitting on her left, and Alec knew with stunning clarity that good ole decade-older Bob wasn't just a last-minute guest of the Sorensens.

The reason Steph hadn't just *told* him she'd asked someone else to be her escort was no doubt due to some twisted feminine logic that he didn't care to untwist. It simply wasn't worth the effort to him. Now, if it had been Gwen...well, it should have been Gwen, damn it.

He pulled into her parking spot—the one she was entitled to. The jerk from across the way was apparently out tonight.

He had fun with Gwen. Her logic was rarely twisted, and when it was, he only had to verbally spin her around once the other way, and all was well.

Okay, maybe Gwen did talk too much sometimes, but she...she was now looking at him with a wide-eyed expression bordering on panic.

"Because I'm packing turkey and ham."

"What?" Maybe it was just his night for twisted feminine logic.

"What you just said about New Year's Eve—it's because of the turkey and the ham, right?" Her voice sounded strange.

Alec turned off the car. There was silence except for the faint popping of fireworks. "Not *just* because of the turkey and the ham." He wanted to tell her...what? That when his evening had begun to go south, all he could think about was sitting on her couch with the world's largest bowl of popcorn and chanting Scooby-Doo dialogue with her?

The silence thickened.

He couldn't read the expression in her eyes. Or maybe he could and he didn't want to. Because maybe the same expression was in *his* eyes. Better not go there. "There's also the champagne and the rolls and the pickles and the salmon and the cheese—"

"Oh, well, yes." She looked relieved and he relaxed. "That goes without saying."

"I like saying it. I'm hungry."

"Then help me unload all this stuff and I'll make you a sandwich."

They both got out of the car.

"Just one?" Alec asked.

...ded him a sack. "It'll be one heck of a

A MINUTE there she'd thought...but that would have been stupid. So, so stupid. And embarrassing. And counter to her goals.

Honestly. People kept making the same mistakes over and over and never could see them. Gwen felt very clever and mature that she'd even recognized her pattern of picking high-maintenance men and that it was affecting her relationships with them in the workplace. It had to stop. She was trying to change and yet, she could feel herself drawn to Alec even though she knew she'd just be making the same mistakes all over again.

It must be the chocolate theory of dieting. Even thinking the word "diet" brought on cravings for the very foods that had to be avoided.

"Hey, hurry up," Alec said from behind her on the stairs. "It's almost midnight."

"So?" Gwen asked grumpily.

"So, fireworks. If we climb up to the roof, we can see Astroworld." Alec still had her keys and opened her door.

They headed for the kitchen and dumped the packages on the bar. "I'll unload the rest of the stuff and you can make the sandwiches."

"Heaven forbid I should let a man go hungry while it's within my power to feed him," Gwen continued to grumble as she ripped open a sack of rolls and cut the plastic off the ham, then peeled away the heavy foil.

She was slathering mustard on a roll half when she heard footsteps resonating in the outside hall.

"Hurry, hurry, hurry." Alec literally ran into the room, dumped the sacks, tore off a paper towel and wrapped up his half-finished sandwich. "Grab the champagne and go. I'll get glasses."

"Go where?"

"Fire escape."

Gwen wasn't sure she wanted to climb up the fire escape, but Alec had slammed her cupboard and was barreling toward her, so Gwen ran out the door in self-defense.

"Are you sure it'll hold me?" she asked as Alec pulled down the bottom part of the metal ladder.

"That would be the point of a fire escape. Besides, people go up here all the time. It's a great place to sunbathe."

Gwen slowly placed her feet on the metal rungs, being careful not to catch her heels in the grid. "Sunbathing is bad for you." Like she would ever expose her large, white thighs to Alec's eyes.

Speaking of, she just wouldn't think about him behind her on the ladder. Since she lived on the upper floor, it was a relatively short climb to the flat roof. They weren't the only ones who'd come up there to watch the fireworks, but the other residents were clustered on the far end.

Alec joined her on the roof and headed for a large square air-conditioning unit and set the glasses and paper-towel wrapped sandwich on top. He shoved back his sleeve and checked his watch. "Forty-five seconds."

Ripping off the foil of the champagne bottle, he unwound the cage and carefully, but expertly removed the cork. It popped, but only a thread of vapor rose from the lip. "We don't want to waste the good stuff." He poured two glasses and handed her one.

Gwen watched the champagne bubble up to the rim without dripping over. "*Veuve Clicquot* champagne in Scooby-Doo jelly jar glasses?"

"That says something about us, doesn't it?"

"Yes, but I don't know what."

"Ten! Nine! Eight..." The crowd on the far edge of the roof began a countdown.

His hand in the small of her back, Alec maneuvered Gwen until she was facing the southeast. She was just in time to see an explosion of fireworks over the Astrodome complex and more in the distance, outlining the Houston skyline.

"Happy New Year." Alec clinked her Scooby-Doo glass with his.

Gwen clinked back and started to drink, then noticed Alec gazing at her, his mouth curved in the slightest of smiles.

The amazing thing about facial features and expressions was that millimeters made all the difference between beauty and ordinariness and, in this case, friendly and unutterably sexy.

A few millimeters more and Alec's intimate smile would have widened into a grin and his smoldering eyes would have crinkled with friendliness.

But those few millimeters weren't there and as a result, Alec was, it had to be acknowledged—though Gwen would really rather not—sex on the hoof.

Maybe he didn't even know it. Maybe it was just that he was so good-looking he couldn't help himself. He was on automatic pilot. That was it. The props were all present: midnight on New Year's Eve, champagne, the tux, the sky bursting into color all around them....

Except those were her kind of props, weren't they? She was reading way more into his expression than she should. They were drinking out of jelly glasses with cartoon characters on them, for pity's sake.

And yet...it was midnight on New Year's Eve after all. Who a person was with at that time was important, right? Alec had said he'd wanted to be with her and he was and he'd returned *before* he'd known about the ham and turkey. So there.

Yes, there. Or, rather, here. That look on his face... Gwen muffled a whimper. She felt like she was one of the bad girls in a 007 movie, the women who were drawn to James even though they knew he was the enemy.

All this awareness and rationalizing and denying took place in that split second after Gwen lifted the glass to her lips and tilted it back—that split second when her mind should have been automatically calculating the amount of tilt and resulting volume of liquid likely to enter her mouth and was instead occupied with Alec.

As a result, she took a too-large swallow and felt champagne bubbles explode in her nose.

"Yeah, we let it get a little warm." Alec thumped her on the back. Of course it was in a very sexy...no. Not sexy at all. Thumping, in fact, as though she were a fellow linebacker in a pickup football game who had done a really good linebacker kind of thing.

Gwen held up a hand. "I'm okay."

"Champagne was what got me into trouble tonight, too."

"Really?" Gwen tried an experimental sip and hoped she sounded casual and I'm-interested-only-if-you-feel-like-talking-about-it when she was no such thing.

"Steph expected me to buy champagne for our table."

"And you couldn't afford to."

"Not at this time."

"And she didn't understand." *Shut up and let him talk.*

"No. It wasn't her fault."

Yes it was. Yes it was.

"When I showed up, she assumed I was making an exception to the poverty rule."

"Didn't you explain?"

He shook his head. "Nah."

"Maybe if you'd—"

"It wouldn't have mattered."

Thank heavens he'd shut her up before she'd managed to patch up his relationship. Not that it mattered... Gwen sighed. Heavily and loudly. Then she mentally reminded herself—one more time—that even if Alec were free, she wasn't his type. And even if he *were* attracted to her, she'd spend all her time trying to keep the relationship going at the expense of her personal goals.

With her, there appeared to be no happy medium.

Look what he'd done to Stephanie. She'd worked on this big charity deal and Alec hadn't paid any attention to it. He wouldn't even have attended if Gwen hadn't figured out a way for him to do so. Did she really, truly think he'd act any differently toward her?

"GWEN, I APPRECIATE your support, but Steph has moved on and I'm fine with that."

Gwen had sounded so disgusted with him. Truthfully, he was disgusted with himself. Sure, and Steph, too. But it was more his fault than hers.

"I'm sorry," she said.

"So am I, but not a lot, you know?"

She took a sip of the champagne. "Not really."

Gwen was watching the last of the fireworks and not paying much attention to him. Maybe that's why he found himself in a talkative mood.

"I'm not the same person I was when we started dating, and that's not fair to her."

"What kind of person were you?"

"Oh, you know."

"No, Alec, I don't." She walked over to the air-conditioning unit and perched on it.

"That's right. You didn't know me before I came to live here." He topped off her glass and refilled his own. "I guess you could say I lived the good life. I worked hard, ate out every night. Went to plays, clubs, drove a nice car, had a membership at the Racquet Club, lived in a great place—"

"Dated a lot of women."

"I wasn't going to say that."

"You didn't have to."

It didn't sound like a compliment. Alec set down his glass and unwrapped the sandwich. Tearing off a hunk, he handed it to her. She took it and they both chewed thoughtfully.

At least Alec was chewing thoughtfully. He wouldn't presume to know what Gwen was thinking. "I'm not going to apologize for dating."

She turned to him. "What makes you think I expect you to?"

"Well…you aren't saying anything."

"It's not polite to talk with your mouth full."

"Your mouth isn't full now."

"Okay."

Alec didn't like the way that "okay" sounded.

"It seems to me that the only way you've changed is that you aren't making as much money."

"That's part of it," he agreed cautiously.

"Sounds to me like that's all of it."

"Maybe it is. All I know is that I look at things—at life—differently now."

"In other words, slumming makes you feel noble."

"Hey…I never said that!"

She set her glass down and drew her arms around herself. "You know, Alec, I may not eat out every night, or drive a fancy car—and you know where I live—but I think I have a pretty good life."

"And women wonder why men never want to *talk*."

"Okay, let's back up—do you or do you not believe that Stephanie dropped you—"

"I'm the one who left!"

"Fine, whatever. Did your lack of money cause your breakup?"

"My lack of money is temporary. But you know what it was? Money fueled a busy life for me. I was always doing something or was always with people. I don't want to say my life was shallow, except that I never took time to think. And you know something else? I was really good in business because I wasn't afraid to take risks. I didn't have to play it safe because if I failed, the family would be a safety net. Sure, there'd be consequences, but starvation wasn't one of them. Losing my home wasn't either. Neither was getting fired. Now, I've got to think and rethink every decision, because if I make a mistake, that's it. Game over."

"You're not going to starve now, either."

"No, but I'm playing by those rules. I'm a different person because of it."

She was staring at him, shivering slightly.

"Oh, hey." He shrugged out of his jacket and draped it around her shoulders.

"How gallant of you. Thanks."

"I dragged you up here without a jacket."

"I wouldn't have missed it."

"Yeah, well, sorry about the lecture."

"I wouldn't have missed that, either."

She wore a wry smile, and her voice was lower and huskier than usual. It caught his attention in a way he normally didn't associate with Gwen.

As he watched, she reached back and pulled her hair out from under his coat, shook her head, then pulled the lapels tighter across her chest, burrowing deeper in his coat.

Alec's breath caught somewhere between his chest and his throat.

Fortunately, she was unaware that he was staring at her because her attention was on the occasional contraband bottle rockets and Roman candles being launched from area parking lots below them.

For some odd reason, Gwen looked really good in green and red light. Her eyes appeared larger and darker than usual, and the flickering shadow patterns gave her face, what he could see of it above his jacket collar, a more angular, mysterious look.

She was stunningly attractive. Actually, the stunned part referred to Alec. This was Gwen, after all. Not that she'd ever been hard on the eyes, but...well, hey. She should stand under fireworks more often.

There was a breeze up on the flat roof and as Gwen took another sip of champagne, a piece of her hair whipped across her cheek and curled around the glass.

Alec reached out. At that moment, her eyes swiveled his way. What was he doing? He checked the movement, then continued, because if he stopped, it would draw attention to what he was doing and Gwen would know something was wrong. Not that anything was wrong. Yet.

Alec caught the piece of hair, tugged it away from the glass and smoothed it around her ear. It had been an excuse to touch her. He hoped she didn't realize it.

She smiled and retucked the hair around her ear, then did the other side, as well. She looked more like Gwen now and less like...like *not* Gwen.

"Aren't you cold?" she asked, giving a little shiver.

"No." Ha.

She dipped her head, then sniffed at his lapel. "Poison."

"Pardon?"

"I smell perfume. Poison."

"Stephanie's perfume." Which she'd worn for another man. "We danced."

"Did you have a good band?"

"Yes." He was going to have to do better than that in the conversation department. "No 'Muskrat Love.'"

She smiled. She had a nice smile. "The melody kind of grows on you."

Apparently that wasn't the only thing. Alec swallowed. "Steph had a backup date."

Gwen didn't even blink at his change of subject. "How awful. Though I must admit it was smart of her, but awkward for you."

"*He* bought the champagne for the table and I gracefully departed from the field."

"Poor you."

"No, I'm glad I went. It helped me get things straight in my head." Only now other things were getting mixed up.

"What things?"

"Like Stephanie and I weren't cut out for longterm."

She rolled her eyes. "Does any man *ever* look at a woman and think 'long-term'?"

Alec glanced at her, then looked quickly away. Fortunately, someone launched a bottle rocket from their parking lot just then and it went whizzing up through the trees. He hoped Gwen, if she noticed that he didn't meet her eyes, would attribute it to that.

He should have known better.

"Look at you! Even hearing the word 'long-term' makes you nervous!"

"No." Now he did look at her. "It was the thought of long-term with *Steph*." He'd realized that this evening and it wasn't just at the charity gala. It was being here, on the roof with Gwen, too.

A string of firecrackers went off close by and she jumped, briefly knocking against him.

His arm automatically came around to steady her. Automatically, because he'd been wanting to touch her again for the past few minutes and trying to talk himself out of it. This seemed like fate.

The firecrackers had been set off by the crowd over at the other end of the roof. The people were laughing and running toward the stairs at their end.

"Someone is bound to call the police after that," Gwen remarked.

She shivered slightly, or at least Alec liked to think so. He kept his arm around her. Purely for warmth.

"You're cold. Here." Before he could stop her, Gwen opened up his jacket and offered him half.

He should refuse. He should suggest they go inside.

He scooted closer to her and put the jacket over his shoulder where it did very little good except to get him closer to Gwen.

But he was a grown man. He could have impulses and not act on them. Acting on them would ruin a perfectly good friendship and embarrass them both.

Gwen didn't see him as boyfriend material. He knew that because he knew how women who were interested in him acted. Gwen didn't act that way, thank

God. Taking away that element between them took the pressure off. It was so *easy* to be with her. And when he wasn't, he didn't have to worry that she was on the phone with her girlfriends dissecting his actions and what impact they had on their *relationship*.

She smiled up at him. The parking lot lights were reflected in her eyes. If he were the poetic sort—and he most definitely was not—he'd think they looked like stars in her eyes.

She felt good next to him. Soft and warm.

And that smile... Gwen had a nice set of lips on her.

He bent his head and she stilled.

Hell. Now look what he'd done.

This was Gwen. *Gwen.* He couldn't do this. He shouldn't do this. He *wouldn't* do this.

"You've been great," he murmured. "I really needed a friend tonight." And then he changed trajectories and placed a chaste kiss on her cheek. "Happy New Year."

6

FRIEND. *FRIEND. F-R-I-E-N-D* friend. Amazing how one little six-letter word put everything into perspective.

Gwen had actually thought he was about to kiss her. And not any of this peck-on-the-cheek stuff, either. Really kiss her. She could have sworn he was wearing an I'm-about-to-kiss-you look. Her body had thought it had received a good-to-go signal. Her heart had picked up speed. She may have tilted her head. She'd certainly moistened her lips.

And then her ears had picked up on the word "friend." They hadn't transmitted this info to her body in time to avoid the little zing she got from the feel of his lips on her cheek, but all body parts concerned eventually got the message in time to wish him a casual, "Happy New Year" back.

Friend. That was wisest, truly. And she was fine with that, really. Had they engaged in a serious lip lock, it would have been a classic case of rebound on his part and a classic case of stupidity on her part.

Therefore, as a friendly gesture, when they climbed off the roof, she'd packed up leftovers and insisted he take them with him, rather than going with her original plan of inviting him to eat them with her in her apartment over the next week.

He seemed a little taken aback with the abundance

of food, but she waved him off with a cheery, "That's what friends are for!"

And New Year's Day, when Alec came around hoping to watch football on cable, she was able to greet him in a friendly sort of way, offering to let him watch whatever he wanted. After all, she was going to vacuum, so he wouldn't bother her. Nope, not at all.

Gwen vacuumed her bedroom floor, her closet, the shelves, the valance, the miniblinds and the dust ruffle on her bed. She vacuumed her chair, though it usually was covered with clothes and didn't get very dusty. Then, she hauled the vacuum cleaner into the living room and went after the floor, the drapes, and then had her friend, Alec, help her move the sofa so she could vacuum beneath it.

Her friend Alec left before halftime.

Gwen was sorry to see him go and angry with herself for feeling that way. She was horribly conflicted between doing the right thing—concentrating on her career, which would raise her standard of living—and wanting the wrong thing—Alec, who'd be fun, but would probably result in heartache and eventually leave her where she began, except a few pounds heavier from the ice cream she'd eat to cope with the inevitable breakup.

In the past, she'd wanted the right thing, but had done the wrong thing. And as wonderfully hunky and desirable as her friendly neighbor was, he was the Wrong Thing personified.

This was a new year and she resolved to change. She might want the wrong thing, but she was bound and determined to do the right thing.

And speaking of resolutions, there was the skirt. Suppose there was something to the legend about it attracting the right man. Was there any real harm in losing a few pounds until she could zip it up? It would be humiliating to confess to Chelsea and Kate that she couldn't get into the skirt.

Besides, then she could wear it in front of Alec and when nothing happened, she'd feel better about having done the right thing, which was sticking to her good-neighbor-only policy where he was concerned.

So that night, in the splendor of her newly vacuumed apartment, she concentrated on her plan for work. And the next day, she put those plans into action by calling for quotes for unbleached coffee filters.

Unfortunately, since New Year's fell midweek, most people had just taken the whole week off and Gwen ended up leaving messages on voice mail and e-mail.

Never mind. She spent the two days organizing her files and cleaning off her desk. She ate salad for lunch—dressing on the side. She gave up ice cream, even though it had been an extremely ice creamy week.

And did the skirt allow her to zip it up? No.

She wasn't actually going to have to do sit-ups, was she?

Friday after work, Gwen wandered into the kitchen and opened the door of her leftover laden freezer. She could really use some ice cream. It was Friday night, after all. Just a tiny pint. She wouldn't eat it all...

The phone rang just as she was getting her jacket and purse, having decided that if she walked to the Quick Mart, the calories expended would cancel out the calories consumed. Gwen hesitated, then answered the phone, hoping it was Alec, despising herself for the hope, and knowing it wasn't because he usually dropped by unannounced.

It was her mother. "Gwen? Your father has departed for the great Northwest."

Gwen blinked. "You're kidding?"

"Not after two days, I'm not."

Guilt slammed into her. She hadn't forgotten about her father and his back-to-nature craze, exactly, but she'd thought that her parents would work everything out and their lives would go back to normal. When she hadn't heard otherwise, she'd assumed that's what had happened.

"He couldn't have left, Mom. He didn't say goodbye."

There was a telling silence.

"He's gone? Really?"

"Yes."

She may have been a grown woman, but Gwen felt a very raw childish hurt. Her father had left without saying goodbye to her?

It was such a man thing to do. She'd never thought of her father as a *man* man before, but that's what he was, wasn't he?

Oh, her poor mother. Her mother had joined the ranks of rejected females everywhere. Gwen could relate. Her mother was...a woman. That was harder to relate to, but Gwen had every intention of trying.

Her head hurt and briefly she wondered if a person could get withdrawal headaches from ice cream like the ones coffee was known for. "Do you want me to come over, Mom?"

"Oh, no!" There was a tinkly laugh, in which Gwen heard a determined breezy cheerfulness. "I mean, if *you* want to come over, then I'd love to see you, but don't feel you *must* come over."

"I feel I should come over."

Another tinkly laugh. "Actually, I'm on my cell phone in your parking lot...I—I was on my way to bridge, you know we have a standing game the first Friday night of the month with the Brillsteins and it was more habit than anything, but without Tom, we'll lack a fourth, so I canceled."

Gwen thought she heard a vocal quiver. "Come on up, Mom. I was just about to make myself a ham sandwich."

"Not ham, I think. I'm bloating."

Gwen hung up the phone, poised to make a last-minute dash and grab through her apartment, but found herself in the novel position of having her mother drop in when her apartment was actually clean. What were the chances?

Then, again, what were the chances of spending Friday night with her mother? Not that she didn't get along with her mother if they avoided discussing lifestyles and posture, but theirs was more of a lunch relationship, not a Friday night relationship.

Gwen went into the kitchen and put a saucepan with water on to boil. She'd forgotten about her teakettle one day and it had burnt up. Green tea should be just the thing to offer a hysterical parent with bloating.

She heard her mother's footsteps echoing on the concrete and metal stairs outside. Gwen pulled out a couple of tissues, then decided to take the whole box and headed toward the door just as her mother knocked. Gwen opened the door, expecting sobbing hysteria.

In walked her mother. "Hi, Gwen! I'm so glad you're home."

There was no sobbing and very little hysteria.

Gwen set the box of tissues on top of her TV and closed the door behind her mother.

"I can't remember the last time it was just us girls."

"It was lunch last month." They'd met in the Neiman-Marcus china department and Gwen had had to endure her mother pointing out the china, silver and crystal patterns selected by the offspring of her various friends. Gwen offered to choose a china pattern, too, but apparently single people didn't do that sort of thing.

"So it was." Suzanne gestured to Gwen's coat. "You were going out."

"Just for ice cream," Gwen admitted.

"Have you eaten dinner?"

"No."

Suzanne looked at her, then around at her apartment. "The ice cream *was* your dinner, wasn't it?"

"Um...not on purpose."

Waving away Gwen's explanation, Suzanne slumped. It was the first time Gwen ever remembered seeing her mother do so.

Stand up straight, Gwen. Slouching is defeatist and weak. You must present a strong, confident image—even when you're wrong. Especially when you're wrong.

Gwen took off her coat and threw back her shoulders, ready to rally her mother.

"There have been times when *I* wanted to have ice

cream for dinner, but there was always your father..."
Suzanne exhaled and straightened her shoulders. "But
did he appreciate all I've done? No. Without so much
as a by-your-leave, he quits his job, packs and takes
off."

She sat on the sofa, but Gwen thought it looked more
like her knees just gave out.

"I don't even know if he's got enough socks—he's
never packed for himself in his life. But he's no longer
my concern."

The saucepan lid rattled and Gwen went to make the
tea. She turned off the stove and put two tea bags into
mugs, then poured the water.

"You were right all along, Gwen," her mother called
from the sofa. "You said I was living your worst nightmare and you were right."

Gwen nearly poured boiling water over her hand.
She hadn't said that, had she? She'd certainly *thought* it,
but had she actually said the words to her mother?
Bad. Very bad.

"I thought Tom and I had an equal partnership. I
thought we were being so clever. Instead of both of us
working hard at two jobs, the way everybody else did,
we worked hard at one job—his. And we were such a
success—just blew away the competition. He told me
that people had asked him what his secret was. *I* was
his secret."

And she never got any of the credit, which was exactly Gwen's point. However, now was not the time to
make that point.

"My entire married life, I've considered my position
as Tom's wife before I did anything. I shopped at the

right grocery stores, I used the right caterer and decorator and I certainly never bought any clothes without considering my image. Our goal was to be the perfect corporate package."

Gwen set a mug of tea in front of her mother and gingerly sat next to her on the sofa.

"That package is now unwrapped," Suzanne stated.

Her mother was just venting. Gwen had both vented and been the ventee enough times with Laurie and others to know that her role was to offer sympathy and agreement.

But this was her *mother* talking about her *father*. Maybe she should bend the rules. "Dad will come back. You know he will. He's just—"

"In El Paso." Her mother took an experimental sip of tea, which was still pretty hot.

"What?"

"Or at least that's where he was at lunchtime when he called." Suzanne looked around for a coaster and when she didn't find one, pulled the newspaper's television guide from the stack on Gwen's coffee table and set the mug on it. "He wanted to know if he'd left his solar-powered lantern in the garage. I told him he could come back and look for himself."

"Mom!"

"He's on his own," she reiterated. "And I'm ready to start living for myself, just the way you do."

"Well, Mom..." Gwen had a horrible thought. Her mother wasn't intimating that they hang out together, was she?

"After all, I'm only fifty. My life is hardly over. You know what they say—fifty is nifty."

"Well, no, I didn't know that."

"Still..." Her mother was looking at her in an assessing way. "If I'm going to be back on the market, then I'll need some repackaging." She jumped up, so Gwen did, too.

"I want to look through your closet to see what you younger girls are wearing."

"Mom?" Back on the market? No. Wrong. Did not compute. "Don't you think it's too soon to—"

But Suzanne had abandoned her sedate green tea and was headed for Gwen's closet. She had the doors open before Gwen could scramble around the sofa after her.

Even worse, she'd pawed through Gwen's "fat" clothes and was already into the back where the "when the devil ice-skates" clothes were. "Here we go. These must be your date clothes. Hmm. Short and tight—just what I need."

"Mom!"

"Honey, I dated through the sixties. We knew short. This is a cute top." She pulled out a see-through chiffon blouse that Gwen had bought during the last of the Eric days when she'd been trying to rekindle something that had no business being rekindled.

Suzanne pulled out another hanger. "And this must be the tank you wear under it."

Well, no, it wasn't, but Gwen had no intention of correcting her mother. Besides, at that moment, her mother drew out the skirt—the skirt that Gwen had given up ice cream for.

"This makes a cute outfit, don't you think?" Suzanne held the three pieces together. "Can I borrow it?"

"No!"

Suzanne had already started undressing. "Why not?"

"Because." Gwen eyed the skirt nervously. What were the rules in a situation like this? "You just...what are you doing?"

"Changing clothes. I want to go out."

"Out where?" Gwen asked suspiciously.

"You know. Out. And I'll need the right clothes."

"But you can't wear that!"

Suzanne stepped out of her skirt and pulled on the black one. Effortlessly.

Then she zipped it shut. Easily. "Oh, I like this." She twirled from side to side and the skirt lovingly caressed her legs. "The fabric is wonderful. Where did you get it?"

"A friend," Gwen mumbled, glaring at the traitorous skirt.

"It's got a certain something, doesn't?"

"You have no idea."

And then, to Gwen's horror, her mother peeled off her sedate blouse and *took off her bra* before putting on the tank top and blouse over it. "What are you doing!"

Suzanne laughed. "Only the young can pull off the visible bra strap look. The rest of us look sloppy."

Gwen spluttered.

"Relax. We used to go braless all the time."

The key words being "used to." And "mother." That was an important key word, too.

"There. How do I look?"

"Um..." Actually, pretty good. Gwen glared at the skirt again.

Her mother misinterpreted Gwen's expression. "Oh, my hair. It's too country clubish, right?"

"Yes." Gwen seized the excuse. Now maybe her mother would forget about doing whatever she was getting ready to do. "Ruins the whole look. You'll have to..." Gwen trailed off as Suzanne made for the bathroom where she vigorously brushed out her hair.

Her mother's hair had always been a blond-streaked, hair-sprayed work of art. Gwen was afraid it had forgotten how to move.

"How's that?" Suzanne turned to her.

"It's depoufed all right." She looked so different.

Her mother tucked her hair behind her ears. It made her look younger in a very non-motherly sort of way.

"There." Suzanne studied her reflection, then gave a satisfied smile. "Now, where is the hottest, hippest club around?"

Gwen didn't know firsthand. Since she'd given up men, she'd also given up the club scene. Laurie, however, hadn't. "Fletchers on Richmond. But you need to know someone." Perfect. Her mother would never get in.

Her mother gave her a dangerous smile and strutted out of the bedroom. "So I'll make friends with the dude at the door."

Gwen winced. "Mom..." She ran after her. "Wait. I'll go with you. It'll—it'll be fun." Lightning couldn't strike indoors, could it?

Suzanne shrugged into her coat. "Gwen, sweetie, I hope you don't take this the wrong way, but a woman with a child doesn't have as good a chance of attracting a man."

"I'm twenty-six!"

But her mother was already out the door—wearing the skirt.

Gwen hesitated. What if that stupid skirt really did have some sort of man-attracting powers? Her *mother* was wearing it. She'd better go after her.

Grabbing her purse and keys, Gwen flung open the door—and ran right into Alec.

"Hi."

One look at his face and Gwen figured her mother was old enough to take care of herself.

"What's wrong?"

He tried a smile and failed. "Gee, you mean it shows?"

"Yes. You look awful. Come in."

Frowning, he still stood at the doorway, hands shoved into the pockets of his disreputable shorts. Shorts and T-shirt. No jacket. Running shoes with no socks. Utterly and absolutely adorable. It was so not fair.

"But you're going someplace."

"Not anymore. Get in here." Gwen left the door open and flung her purse toward the TV set.

"Thanks, Gwen." Exhaling, he collapsed on the sofa, leaned his head back and closed his eyes.

"I'm a real pal, yeah, I know." Gwen removed her mother's mug of green tea and carried it into the kitchen. She would have offered Alec some, but he didn't look like he was in a green tea mood.

Taking off her coat after her second abortive attempt to leave, Gwen hung it in the closet. It didn't look like she would be going anywhere soon. "Okay, talk." She settled on the far edge of the sofa, though with Alec sprawling all over, she wasn't that far away.

"Just a setback. A big one. I'd like to get drunk, but I don't have enough money."

"Wow, and you thought of me and my fab anesthetizing talents."

He opened his eyes and stared at the ceiling. "I'd better go."

"No!" Startled, Gwen grasped his arm. This was worse than she thought. "Tell me."

His arm flexed and she released it. "I lined up a manufacturer who's done business with my family before, but since I'm out on my own, the guy wants a deposit. Reasonable, right?"

Gwen nodded.

"But I don't have the money."

Gwen stopped herself from asking how much he needed just in time.

"I applied for a loan, but I played fair and filled out the application with my current financial picture and the bank turned me down. I figured it was because they wanted access to my assets, so I went to another bank."

"And they turned you down, too."

"Yeah, but they wanted to see market research. But I can't get market research without equipment and I can't manufacture equipment without a loan. You know, my grandfather started out with a cart and pastries his landlady baked and he personally wheeled them around the office buildings. A cart is a hell of a lot easier to get than exercise equipment."

"What about the exercise equipment you have now?"

"I can't move it around, for one thing, and for another, I need my own design—which I've got."

"Did you show them your design?"

"Yeah. They were underwhelmed."

"Maybe you'd better tell me more about your business."

The discouraged look faded from his face as he began to talk. Scraping his hair back from his forehead, he gestured with his hands, but the best part was watching him flex various groups of muscles as he talked about exercises to counter the long hours office workers sat at their desks.

"Just give me ten minutes a day."

Gwen roused herself from fantasies in which she'd given Alec way more than ten minutes a day. "That's all it would take?"

"We're not talking competing for Mr. Universe here. We're talking improved health."

"But ten minutes?"

"Over five days, that's fifty minutes. Nearly an hour of exercise that person wouldn't get otherwise. I'm not going after the gym rats. My target market is those people who know they should get some exercise, but can't take the time to drive to the gym after work, change clothes, do a fifteen-minute warm-up, then hit the machines for thirty to forty-five minutes—longer if the gym's crowded—then back on the treadmill for another thirty minutes, then the half-hour drive home and it's late and dinner's not ready and the kids are cranky. And forget it if there's soccer practice or a base-ball game. It's just not going to happen."

"Who's going to be fixing dinner?"

"What?"

Gwen gazed levelly at him. "I asked who was going to fix the dinner? And the kids—who picked them up from soccer practice?"

"I don't know, maybe the car pool."

"Oh." She looked thoughtful. "And who drives the car pool?"

"GWEN—" Alec suddenly realized he'd wandered into a verbal minefield. He'd been on a roll, too. Gwen was such perfect infomercial material—when he could afford an infomercial—that he'd been spouting the script he'd been writing at her and she'd been responding just as he'd written right up to the last bit there. She was supposed to say something like, "But what else can they do?" and he'd tell her. But instead she'd tried to sort out the familial division of labor.

"Maybe nobody drives the car pool. Maybe they forgot because they were at the gym. But they wouldn't have been if they'd spent ten minutes with my program," Alec said in a futile effort to wrestle the conversation back on track.

"The ten minutes, right." Gwen's laugh held no humor. "I'm sorry. I was distracted by the wonderful life you'd described."

Uh-oh, hidden issues. "It's a typical life," he said cautiously. "Not a lot of downtime and opportunity for exercise."

"It doesn't sound like there's time for anything except work and kids."

"People who are living that kind of life assure me that it's exhausting, but rewarding," he said cautiously.

"Tell me, are any of them women?"

Come to think of it, no. "I can't remember."

"The part about cranky kids and fixing dinner...that could be a woman speaking."

"Women don't have a monopoly on cranky kids."

"They've got a monopoly on dealing with them, though."

"Hey!"

"Oh, come on. Just the thought of the life you described is what puts men off marriage."

"Not all men."

"Name one."

"*I'm* not against marriage." He just wasn't ready, yet.

"Uh-huh."

"I'm not!"

"What about Stephanie?"

"What about her?"

"Once you realized she was serious about you couple wise, to the point of expecting you to support her at that charity thing, you, let me see, what were the words? *Departed from the field.*"

"I believe that was *gracefully* departed from the field."

"Emphasis on *departed*." Gwen's mouth had a cynical twist. Either that or the vile-looking stuff she was drinking tasted really nasty.

Alec thought about what she'd said anyway. Had he missed the nesting signs with Steph or had he ignored them? Maybe a little of both. "I'm not against marriage and family," he told Gwen, realizing it was true. "I'm just against marriage and family with *her*."

She looked up at him, eyes wide, then stared into her cup and swirled the dregs of...was that tea?

"What about you?" he asked when she didn't say anything.

"I don't think I'd want to marry her, either."

"Come on...don't you hear the ticking of your biological clock?"

"It went off once when I turned twenty-five, but I hit the snooze button for another five years."

Gwen didn't have a boyfriend, he knew. He'd heard bits and pieces about an Eric, but as far as he knew, she hadn't dated anyone since he'd come to live there. "I'm not hearing a whole lot of enthusiasm."

"Okay." She thunked her mug on the table and crossed her arms in the classic closed posture. "I'm all for marriage and kids. But I am *not* for the man-gets-to-continue-his-career-and-woman-turns-into-a-house-slave scenario."

"Who would be?"

"Hold that thought for when you have a wife and kids."

"Okay."

She eyed him suspiciously. "Sure, it's easy to say *now*—"

"Hey, hey. I want to know how we got from *my* business reversals to *your* beef with guys who don't pull their own parental weight." He held up his index finger. "And speaking of weight, did you know that just ten minutes a day can—"

Gwen collapsed in a fit of laughter, which was a lot better than a prickly Gwen hugging the arm of the sofa. "You just don't give up, do you?"

"No, I don't give up! I came over here so you could wave your magic wand and solve all my problems."

She was still chuckling. "I don't have a magic wand."

"No, but you've got a brain. Now, come on. There's got to be a way around this."

She didn't let him down. They spent the next several minutes brainstorming and not once did Gwen offer him money, which he'd been afraid she'd do, then get all offended when he turned her down.

Admittedly, he'd already thought of most of the solutions she proposed and he was hoping the most obvious solution would occur to her. In fact, it would be best if it would occur to her without him mentioning it first.

"You said your grandfather started with a single cart—what if you started with a single portable exercise machine and moved it from office to office? Bring it to the people, otherwise they'll just make excuses."

Not a bad idea. "I hadn't thought of doing it that way, but it's easy enough—with the right equipment."

"Haven't you been working on a prototype?"

"Can't you tell?" He flexed his arm, liking the way she watched him. Alec flexed another muscle group, then one on the other side and watched her eyes following the flexing muscles across his chest to his other arm.

"You know," she said slowly, still watching him in a way that really pumped up his ego. "That one bank wanted market research. Haven't you done any?"

Gwen was headed in the right direction.

"Sure, but they want actual subject testing." He extended his legs so she could check out the definition. "Getting people to try my idea is the holdup. I can't just go into an office with a prototype. There are liability issues." He waited.

"Well...how about me? I could be your test subject."

Bingo. "Would you?" He gave her his best salesman smile. "You'd be perfect. You work in an office and you're just the sort of person I'm targeting." He hoped she wouldn't remember how he'd described his target market.

But she did. "In other words, out of shape."

"I was going to say not a gym rat."

Her eyes narrowed. "But you were thinking 'out of shape.'"

"Well, I did hear a little huffing and puffing when we climbed the ladder to the roof."

She swatted him with the sofa pillow. "You did not!"

"Hey, weakling, is that the best you can do?"

Gwen smoothed the pillow back into place. "I wouldn't want to hurt you."

"Hurt me?"

"Yes. I'll bet your job at the pager store doesn't pay medical benefits. That means after I injured you, you'd have to pay the doctor with the insurance from your old job, which would break the rules of your game, not to mention the bones—"

"Come here."

"What?" she asked with an innocent look.

He bent his arms and held them in front of him, fists together. "Try to keep me from moving my arms apart."

"Oh, please."

"Do it—unless you're afraid."

"Ha." The light of battle was in her eyes. Gwen gripped his wrists. "Say when."

"When."

She mashed his arms together. "You aren't even trying!"

Alec gave an experimental push and was surprised to feel his arms separate. He stopped and Gwen screwed up her face with increased effort.

Was she faking? He pushed a little more.

"When do you give up?" she gasped.

"Gwen..."

"Had enough?"

He could feel her muscles quiver. A flush had spread across her cheeks. She was biting her lip.

He looked into her eyes, which were not all that far from his. He glanced at her mouth, which was not all that far from his. His gaze moved lower to her neckline, which gaped open. Her chest was not all that far from his.

Boy-oh-boy-oh-boy.

All he had to do was open his arms and Gwen would fall forward, at which point Alec was pretty sure he'd have to kiss her. A for-real kiss. On the lips. Maybe a little tongue action, too.

Gwen wouldn't appreciate that. She wasn't thinking

about kissing—at least not in connection to him. And he wasn't entirely certain he wanted her thinking that way, either.

Well, yes he was. But it was what happened afterward that he hadn't thought through. And until he did, things had better stay as they were.

He drew in a deep breath, smelling something light and sweet that made him smile.

Gwen saw his smile and redoubled her efforts and Alec thought more about kissing her and redoubled his efforts, as well, until he realized that if Gwen held on long enough, she was going to get kissed.

Okay, time. With far less effort than it took to keep from kissing her, he spread his arms apart so fast that Gwen fell forward and bounced her nose against his chest.

Alec automatically brought his hands to her upper arms, not daring to wrap them around her. "You okay?" he asked, hoping she didn't feel the way his heart raced.

"Of course, I'm okay! Again!"

Not again. He couldn't stand again.

Gwen flipped her hair over her shoulder and raised her hands.

She looked very...kissable. But he knew she wouldn't appreciate hearing that. "How about this time you try to keep me from moving my arms together?"

"Okay, macho man. We can give that muscle group a rest." She braced herself between his arms.

Alec immediately realized his mistake. She was even closer than before and grinning up at him in a way that made him want to do a lot more than kiss her. He brought his arms together, trapping her hands between them.

Gwen gasped at her sudden defeat.

They stared at each other.

All he needed was the slightest sign. A softening in her expression. Licking her lips. Parting her mouth. A gentle sway in his direction. The words, "Kiss me, you fool."

But the sign he got was Gwen tugging on her hands. He instantly let her go.

"You're strong."

She had no idea. Still, it was a great opening for a zinger.

Gratefully, he took it. "And you're not."

"No, duh."

Alec needed to move. Move away from Gwen. Change the mood. Definitely. Change...something before he forgot he was with Gwen. "Hey, don't sit there, put on your exercise gear and let's get started."

7

"NOW?" GWEN STARED at the man who'd made her arms feel like jelly. Who'd made other places feel like jelly, too.

"No time like the present." He jumped to his feet, his leg muscles flexing nicely at near eye level.

"Why are you still sitting on the couch?" he asked from above her.

Other than enjoying the great view? "I like it on the couch."

"You can sit on the couch later. Now it's time to exercise."

Oh, that. Gwen had never been much of an exercise junkie and therefore, lacked the nifty little Spandex outfits the women on the late-night commercials wore. Not that she'd wear them if she had them. "Go back to your apartment, I'll come over when I'm ready."

"You get five—okay, ten minutes before I come back over here and drag you out."

"I could lock my door."

"And I could break it down."

Of that, she had no doubt whatsoever. "But you wouldn't."

The look on his face did not reassure her. "It might be worth the repair bill just to do it."

"You're bluffing. You don't have any money."

"You're right." He reached the door and opened it, making a show of checking its heft and hinges. "But I do have pride," he added quietly before gently shutting the door.

Gwen had pride, too, and she knew it was about to get bruised.

But that was okay. Sure, she'd be starting from scratch, exercise wise, but it was only for ten minutes. What was ten minutes between friends?

It was more than ten minutes later when Gwen, in wrinkled shorts and a T-shirt—what was the point of ironing cotton before packing it away for the winter?— walked down her apartment stairs, across the deserted pool area and entered Alec's hallway. She was just climbing the stairs to his apartment, a place she'd been to less than a handful of times, when the door opened and he stuck his head out.

"Thirteen minutes, missy."

"I forgot to allow travel time."

Gwen was conscious of a little heavy breathing when she reached the top of the stairs. Not all of it could be attributed to the thought of being in Alec's apartment—with Alec. "Where's the cat?"

"Armageddon is under the bed. I shut the door."

"You haven't complained about him in a while."

"Brad gave him catnip for Christmas. I think he's been stoned ever since." Alec gave her a half smile. "The cat, that is, although Brad did look pretty mellow."

The door closed with an audible click. Gwen swallowed her nervousness. "I love what you've done with the place."

All furniture had been pushed toward the walls and tools and exercise equipment dominated the living space. The dinette table was covered with a computer and papers. Gwen figured Alec must eat standing over the sink.

"Yeah, I'll be glad to get back into my own place." He gestured for her to stand by the wall and picked up a nifty-looking camera.

"Mug shots?" Gwen couldn't help noticing that Alec seemed awfully prepared for someone who'd only had ten or so minutes to get ready.

"Before and after photos."

She cringed. "Do we have to?"

"What am I going to put in the brochure?"

"You said market research! You didn't say anything about a brochure."

"Market research paper then."

"Well, okay." She backed up to the white wall.

Alec focused the camera.

"Should I smile?"

"No. You're an unhappy 'before.'" The flash went off.

"A digital camera? Business at the pager store must be good."

"I'm renting all this." Alec adjusted the settings. "Hey, can you stick out your stomach and slump or something? You don't look beforeish enough."

She could quite easily fall for him right then and there, Gwen reflected as she relaxed her stomach and allowed Alec to take unflattering pictures of her. "You're going to put one of those black rectangles over my face, aren't you?"

He twirled a finger and Gwen turned to the side. "If you insist."

"Most definitely. Otherwise someday, like when I'm being confirmed as a Supreme Court Justice or trying to get into the White Briar Country Club or something, these photos could come back to haunt me."

"Okay, I'll smear the pixels. Slouch some more, but try to do it naturally—hey, yeah, lower your head. It makes your chins show up more."

And after falling for him, that comment would make her stand right back up again.

"Can you, um, pull your shirt tighter?"

Gwen looked him right in the eye. "No."

"It was just a thought." Alec set the camera by the computer and waved Gwen over to the table. He picked up a microphone and something else. "Test subject one. January third. Oh, damn."

"That's on the recording," she pointed out.

"I know." He used the computer mouse to move the recording marker backward. "I just remembered that the scales are in the bathroom and I can't open the bedroom door because the cat will freak out."

Gwen had stopped breathing at the word "scales." No way. Not even for Alec.

"Do you know how much you weigh?" he asked.

To the ounce. "Yes."

His pencil was poised over a chart with her name on it. He looked up at her. "Aren't you going to tell me?"

"No."

"Gwen—"

"And if you think *any* woman in your target market

will tell her weight to a complete hunk like you, then your little endeavor is doomed. *Doomed*, I tell you."

He was still bent over the table, eyes on the chart. Gwen saw his mouth twitch. "I'm a complete hunk?"

"As if you didn't know."

"It's nice to hear anyway." He straightened and cleared his throat. "However weight-loss data is a great selling point."

"If there is any weight loss involved, you will be the first to know. I'll keep meticulous records."

"Then that's what we'll do," he said, demonstrating that he knew how to pick his battles. "Okay, hold out your arms." He approached her with a measuring tape.

A measuring tape! That thing was a *measuring tape.* Gwen took a step backward. A large step backward. "What are you doing?"

"Getting your measurements. Oh, come on, Gwen," he said impatiently.

And let this be a lesson to you, she thought, holding out her arm. The next time she felt the urge to make life easier for some man, she'd remember this feeling of total mortification.

But Alec couldn't have been more impersonal as he went about measuring her arms, legs, waist, abdomen, hips—she closed her eyes for that one—and chest. For the chest measurement, he simply let her hold the ends in place and took the reading.

He told her what he was writing on the chart in a flat, unemotional voice, and his movements were quick to the point of brusqueness.

She may have been a stuffed dummy for all the effect

she had on him, which was the way it should be and the way she wanted it—except...well, except nothing.

GWEN WASN'T in as bad a shape as Alec had feared after her inability to provide even a minimal resistance for his arms.

No, not in bad shape at all. Maybe even good shape. She was a little soft with a few extra curves...

Who was he kidding? Gwen, he hoped. Desperately.

Sweat trickled between his shoulder blades with the effort he made not to toss the stupid measuring tape over his shoulder and grab her.

And he'd thought the little episode on her couch had been bad. This was worse. Much, much worse. His fingers were touching her in places he'd never thought about in connection with Gwen before. Oh, sure, he'd automatically given her a cataloging once-over months ago, the way any man would. But since then, she'd just been Gwen.

Why now, after all these months, was she pinging his babe meter?

Whatever had happened on New Year's Eve had made Alec see possibilities and he didn't want to see possibilities because they weren't...possible.

He didn't want to be having any awareness of Gwen as a female. That wasn't what they were about. She'd been a good neighbor, then a buddy and a pal. She'd been the least demanding of any woman he'd been around and he enjoyed spending time with her. It was so easy being with her. And look at the favor she was doing for him now.

Sure, she'd caught him by surprise recently. At New

Year's Eve she hadn't looked half-bad. Pretty good, in fact. Since then, she'd looked more than pretty good, but he didn't want to ruin a great friendship by mucking it up with sex. He knew the drill. They wouldn't be able to just hang out anymore because she'd have "expectations." They all did.

And, it was only fair to admit, he'd have expectations, too.

His expectations were growing, as a matter of fact. Right now.

No big deal on the arm. The waist wasn't too bad, either, though she lifted her shirt and his fingers touched the smooth skin of her stomach. But just briefly—as briefly as he could manage.

He tried not to think as he moved the tape lower and quickly measured her abdomen and hips. But of course, he did think. He nearly forgot to read the tape measure, he was thinking so hard. And what he was thinking was that eventually he was going to have to take a chest measurement.

The best for last, he thought grimly.

Maybe she should take her own chest measurement. Yes. That would be wisest.

It had been a *very* long time since he'd been this close to a woman—dancing with Stephanie didn't count. He'd felt nothing. Once upon a time, he'd been attracted to Stephanie, but he knew now it was a surface attraction. She'd never gotten under his skin.

Gwen had started under his skin.

He'd been looking for Armageddon on one of the first beautiful October Saturdays and when he checked the bushes on that side of the apartment complex, he could hear Scooby-Doo theme music coming from her open window. His guilty pleasure. As he listened, he heard an adult female recite dialogue to the TV and knew he had to meet her.

Impulsively, he'd abandoned the cat and had climbed the stairs. He knocked on the door before he could think of what to say, so when she opened it, he just blurted out the truth, ending with, "So now I'm trying to figure out how to convince you I'm not a murderer so you'll invite me in to watch the rest of that episode."

She'd leaned against the doorjamb. "That's a tough one. You could be a murderer with a cartoon fetish."

"Yeah, I know."

She eyed him. "If you wanted to kill someone, what would be your method of choice?"

"Uh...poison?"

"Why poison? Why not shooting?"

"Don't have a gun."

"Stabbing?"

"Ditto a knife."

"You've got kitchen knives. What do you cook with?"

"I don't cook much."

"Why not hire a hit man?"

"I'm broke."

She nodded thoughtfully. "So how will you dispose of the body?"

"Call the police?"

She opened the door. "Come in. I take comfort in the fact that if you *are* a murderer, you'll be caught immediately."

He grinned and followed her over to the sofa.

"By the way, we won't be eating or drinking," she added.

They'd watched the rest of that episode and three more.

The next day, he'd brought her a bagel in a sack he'd decorated with a skull and crossbones. She made him eat half.

And that, as they say, was the beginning of a beautiful friendship.

He should concentrate on that friendship and not on lips and skin and...and other things.

Right now, he knew she was feeling self-conscious. A couple of times, he felt her flinch when he touched her, but she didn't pull away. These were not the actions of a woman in lust.

Resolved to keep his randy thoughts to himself, he knelt to measure her thigh. "Um..."

She understood and wordlessly pulled up the hem of her shorts. Gooseflesh rose as he drew the tape measure around her thigh. He pretended not to notice, but had to clear his throat before reading off the numbers on the tape measure and jotting them down.

Just her calf to go...and then a potentially awkward moment. Might as well get it out there. "And last, but not least, you'll have to help me with your chest."

Her eyes widened, but Alec just kept talking. Who knows what he said, but it must have been convincing because Gwen held the tape in place and read off the numbers.

"Not bad," he murmured.

"Thank you."

Alec felt the top of his ears grow warm. He hadn't meant to say that aloud. He stared at the chart. "Yeah, not bad at all. You're the perfect candidate for ten minutes a day. Not really out of shape, but could improve with toning." He dared to meet her eyes, not sure of the expression he'd find.

But Gwen wasn't paying any attention to him. She was standing over by his prototype. "I can't even figure out how this works."

Relief coursed through him. "Allow me." Working with the machine would be a thousand times easier than being so close to her. "Now, what is the most important part of the routine?"

"I don't know the routine."

"Right. Hang on." He stretched the computer microphone as far as he could and began recording. "Work on intro. See how you've already helped me? Okay, the most important thing is the warm-up. While I set up the machine, I want you to march in place and swing your arms."

Gwen began marching. "I just thought of something—your clients won't be wearing exercise clothes. Women don't like to sweat in silk."

An image of Gwen in sweaty silk dripped through his mind. "Sweating will be minimal. And they can take off their shoes."

"What about their panty hose? They'll snag."

An image of Gwen slowly peeling off her panty hose floated through his mind. "They can take off their panty hose."

Still marching, Gwen shook her head. "Maybe you

could have those little footie thingies—like they have in the shoe stores."

Alec recorded a note to himself. "Investigate little footie thingies."

"How long will it take you to set up the machine?"

"About a minute."

"Will that minute come out of the ten minutes?"

"No."

"So it's really an eleven-minute workout, then."

Alec shot her a look. "Please don't confuse me with facts. Okay, you're all warmed up—"

"I'm hot."

An image of a hot Gwen scorched his mind.

"Take a seat," he instructed her sternly.

She saluted, then sat down.

"Straddle it."

Gwen swung her leg over and sat facing him. Alec knelt and took hold of her ankle. "Put this foot here and this foot there—kind of wrap your knees around..."

And image of Gwen with her legs wrapped around something—or someone—else sprang to mind.

Alec was getting very irritated with his mind. He needed to concentrate. Gwen was his first live subject and where she had trouble, others would as well. Furthermore, he kept forgetting to recite his script. "To counter those long hours spent sitting in front of a computer, I've concentrated on the abdominals in order to strengthen the support for the lower back, and the neck, shoulders and arms."

"Sounds like a plan."

He moved a cushioned bolster across her chest. "I

want you to hang your arms in front and then lean forward against it." He waited while she got into position. "Now press down with your knees."

Gwen pressed, but nothing happened.

Alec got a wrench and loosened the tension on the bar. It jerked downward.

"Oh! I felt that in my back."

"It's supposed to stretch your back out and keep the muscles from tightening up while increasing circulation to your thighs."

"It feels gooood." Gwen rested her head on the bolster with her eyes closed and began slowly and rhythmically moving knees up and down, while doing her best imitation of Armageddon stretching after a particularly long nap.

"Mmm," she purred after each rep.

Alec felt his mouth go dry. "Yes, well." He swallowed. "Good."

"Oh, it's better than good. People will pay big bucks for this. Ooo..." Her mouth puckered.

He was sweating. "Your sixty seconds are up." Thank, God. "Time for the next position."

"I need more than sixty seconds!"

"You can't have more than sixty seconds!" Alec tugged the bolster out from under her and repositioned her knees to the top of the bar. He moved the bolster back and put her arms beneath. "Now you work the abs. Start pulling."

Gwen pulled, surprise on her face when nothing much happened. She pulled harder, her face crinkled with effort. "I'll have you know that this position is just not working for me."

"I should have started with that position." Actually, he probably should have started with upper torso. He recorded a note. "The other will be a reward."

"It needs more than sixty seconds. Take extra seconds from this position."

"Actually, you aren't...your position isn't..."

She looked at him questioningly.

He was going to have to touch her. Kneeling, he adjusted the width of her arms. "Try that." He made the mistake of looking up. Her face was inches from his. Alec stood so fast, he felt light-headed.

Gwen pulled and her forehead smoothed. "Better." She began that slow rhythmic movement that Alec found so distracting. "So, tell me. What kind of training have you had for this?"

"No formal training, so I've been working with the club trainer to develop the routine."

"He's giving you all this info out of the goodness of his heart?"

"That and an option to buy in as a partner if this thing takes off."

"Alec, I've been working my abs for a heck of a lot more than sixty seconds."

"Sorry. Time for shoulders. Scoot back and grab the bar above you."

Gwen couldn't reach it without standing, but the position of bars kept her from doing so without extricating herself entirely. "I see a problem here."

"Damn," Alec said without heat. "I'll get it." He reached for the bar and brought it down to her.

Gwen held it awkwardly. Obviously, she'd never been one for working out in a gym.

"Not like that. Move your hands—"

"Show me."

But the same design flaw that kept her from standing prevented him from being able to stand next to her without hunching over. There was nothing for him to do but straddle the seat in front of her.

Alec tried to do so with a matter-of-factness that would conceal his reluctance to get so close to her that their knees touched. He kept his eyes on her hand, where he turned her knuckles so her wrist was in a straight line.

His gaze was skimming past her face on the way to the other hand when her unblinking eyes caught and held it.

She was very still and her eyes were very wide and her pupils were very dark.

Alec was close enough to see the sheen across her nose and upper lip. He could feel the heat radiating from her body. Her chest moved, each breath bringing it closer to his.

He was glad one of them was able to breathe, since he was about to pass out from lack of oxygen.

He'd never wanted to kiss a woman so much in his life. But it was even more than that—he wanted her to kiss him back.

"There's too much tension," she whispered.

"You can say that again."

"Aren't you going to adjust it?"

Whoa, baby, could he ever make an adjustment! A smile spread across his face.

"Alec, this isn't funny! The bar is about to rip out my shoulder sockets."

The bar. Alec stood so quickly he banged his head on the metal support.

Gwen gasped and let go of the bar, which shot upward catching Alec on the chin. "Ohmigosh!"

"Stay there!" he ordered when she tried to stand. Gingerly he tested his jaw.

"Are you hurt?"

A knock in the head was just what he'd needed. "I'll live, but I clearly need to address safety issues. Why don't we call it a night?"

"Sure." Her voice was very small and she was looking at the floor as she swung her leg over the seat.

Alec groaned and let go of the top of his head. "Hey, no, Gwen, this is exactly what I wanted to happen."

"Getting creamed in the jaw?"

"Better me than a client." He touched her on the shoulder. "Or you. I'd never forgive myself if I hurt you."

She looked up at him and he slowly let his hand fall away.

They stared at one another until a warning gleam appeared in Gwen's eye. "Good, because I'd never forgive you either!"

8

GWEN PURGED the details of her Friday night exercise session with Alec from her memory, though a few sore muscles prevented her from completely wiping it out.

He was *so* not interested in her, and after her incompetent performance, he clearly was going to stay that way. She found herself dwelling on his clinical detachment—it was enough to send a girl down the path of diets and bikini waxes.

Gwen had given up pretending that she felt no attraction to Alec and didn't want him to feel a reciprocal attraction to her. Of course she did. But it was a good thing he wasn't interested because she'd be tempted to get involved. Even that would be okay if she could keep things fun and light, but she knew Alec too well for a fling. He was too complex to be good fling material. Gwen sighed. She wasn't a fling sort of woman, anyway.

She'd been to one and a half therapy sessions in her life. The half was the result of one appointment getting cut short when the therapist had some sort of therapy emergency. Gwen had heard it involved a frustrated clown and a three-year-old's birthday party, but that wasn't the point. Gwen had already lost faith in the therapist—who'd been Laurie's—anyway.

Laurie was the one who'd suggested she try therapy

after Eric. Not that Gwen had anything against therapy, but when the therapist wanted to spend months exploring Gwen's childhood before hearing about Eric's bad qualities, well, Gwen figured a four-day cruise out of Galveston would do as much good, would cost less and be a lot more fun.

So that's what she and Laurie had done. But one off-hand comment the therapist made had stuck with her—Gwen's need to self-sacrifice probably stemmed from insecurity. But really, didn't everything?

One thing was for sure, she felt a lot more sympathy for women who kept falling for men who were wrong for them—especially since she was one of them.

Resolutely, Gwen picked up her phone and punched the number for Grainier Restaurant Supply. Maybe someday, she mused as she punched her way through the phone system. Someday, when she felt supremely self-secure, she'd tackle Alec. And what better way to boost self-confidence than a promotion with a big, fat pay raise?

"Neil Porter, please. This is Gwen Kempner from Kwik Koffee."

His voice mail picked up. At eight-thirty? Neil, the Kwik Koffee account executive, was clearly not the go-getter Gwen was. She identified herself and left another message requesting a quote on environmentally friendly, unbleached coffee filters.

Gwen had better luck the next three places she called and was inputting the data in a spreadsheet when Laurie knocked on her cubicle door.

"Hey, she lives. What brings you to this side of the building?"

"This." Laurie grinned and tossed a folder with the fourth quarter sales report on Gwen's desk. "At least that's my official excuse. But I really wanted to tell you all about Brian." She dragged one of the extra chairs from the hallway next to Gwen's desk.

Oh, joy. Laurie had disappeared off the face of the earth with Brian after New Year's Eve. And now Gwen was going to be tortured with details, which, judging by Laurie's blissful expression, were going to be many and enviable.

Laurie hugged her knees. "Gwen, he's soooooo wonderful."

Gwen's fingers inched toward the quarterly report. It was released early, since the end-of-year report was being prepared.

"And he's so generous, if you know what I mean."

"No," Gwen answered absently, trying to figure out a way to nonchalantly check where her region was ranked in the sales figures without Laurie noticing.

Laurie leaned toward her, effectively cutting Gwen off from the report. "He has a tongue and he knows how to use it," she murmured with a shiver.

Gwen did not want to have this conversation since she had no new firsthand, er, first-tongue experience to contribute. Prices on unbleached coffee filters didn't compare.

Just to be polite, she listened as Laurie went into details, which were every bit as enviable as she'd suspected, then asked, "So what's wrong with him?"

"Why do you think something's wrong with him?"

"Because something always is," Gwen replied.

"He's outwardly perfect, yet unattached. What's wrong with that picture?"

Laurie frowned, then admitted, "He's a lawyer and works, like, eighty hours a week. He was on vacation last week." She sighed. "I don't know when I'll get to see him again."

"Uh, at night?"

"Maybe. He says that sometimes, a group from his office unwinds at Fletchers. Maybe I can just happen to be there at the same time."

Gwen offered faux sympathy for a few more minutes, then Laurie stood. "I've got to get back to work. I'll warn you, it's grim."

"What is?"

Laurie pointed to the report. "Sales are down."

"Well, yeah, aren't they always at this time? Holidays mean people aren't in the office drinking coffee."

"It's worse than that. I just wanted to give you an early heads-up. This won't go into distribution until after lunch and I guarantee there is going to be a meeting." She waggled her fingers and left.

Gwen pounced on the sales ranking stats, disappointed to see that the Southwest region, hers, was solidly in the middle, just where it had been for the past year.

"Is that the latest quarterly report?" At the sound of her boss's voice, Gwen jumped.

"Yes."

Mr. Eltzburg took it from her. "How did you get it?"

"A friend of mine works in that department. They're distributing them." Laurie wouldn't get in trouble, would she? And then Gwen remembered that she'd vowed to be more aggressive in her professional dealings. "I'm very interested in our sales position, since I work with some of the marketing accounts. We've gone up a percentage point, but still have a long way to go before we take over third place."

"Hmm." Mr. Eltzburg was busy looking for the same rankings Gwen had, and accepted what she'd said without comment. Or maybe he was just stunned. The figures really had been bad.

He stood in her doorway and scanned the report, his face expressionless.

Gwen swallowed. "I believe it's misleading to use gross sales as the only criteria for rank." She paused to give herself a mental pep talk only to find that she'd caught Mr. Eltzburg's attention. He was looking at her, apparently waiting to hear what she had to say. It was such a novel situation she nearly forgot what she'd been about to say. "We're in the southwestern region. It's warmer here! People aren't going to drink as much coffee in the warmer months. The regions with a colder climate will always outsell us."

"Good point." He gave her a thoughtful look before handing the report back to her. "Not that it'll matter when the overall drop in sales gets out. There goes my bonus," he muttered as he left.

Bonus? He got a bonus? All to himself without so much as a box of thank-you donuts for his hardworking staff? When Gwen got her promotion, she vowed to remember her staff.

Her staff had a great sound to it.

With that thought, Gwen picked up the quarterly report. There had to be something in it that she could use. Laurie had said that there was certain to be a meeting.

Gwen was going to be prepared.

COULD ANYTHING possibly be drier reading than a quarterly report?

Arriving home after work, Gwen locked her car and walked across the parking lot to her apartment. Her foot was on the bottom step of the stairs when Alec caught up with her. He seemed to have completely recovered from Friday night. No visible bruises on his handsome jaw. Apparently the only bruises were the ones to Gwen's pride.

He grinned at her. "Ready for round two?"

"You're a glutton for punishment." Striving to keep her breathing even, Gwen started up the stairs.

"That's perseverance and determination. So how about it?" He was so slickly charming, and she was falling for it.

"Do I have to?" she asked, already knowing she would.

"No, you don't *have* to."

"But you'll bug me about it until I do the ten minutes, right?"

"Right."

Gwen rolled her eyes at him and unlocked the door to her apartment. "I'll change."

"I'll fix you dinner afterward—ham."

"Oh, goody."

Gwen changed into the same shorts and T-shirt she'd had on before. When she came out of the bedroom, Alec was reading the TV listings as he sat on one of the kitchen counter stools.

"You're a popular girl these days."

"How so?"

Alec indicated her answering machine. "You've got a potful of messages."

Gwen glanced at the red number: fourteen. Fourteen? She never had that many messages. Momentarily forgetting about Alec, which just demonstrated how truly *rare* getting so many messages was, Gwen punched the play button. There were a couple of hangups, one recording, and eleven messages from her father.

"So he really took off?" Alec's deep voice held a hint of sympathy. Not enough to embarrass her, but enough to show concern, which irritated her for some reason.

"I guess so."

Her father was using the telephone from an old-fashioned general store in some remote little town, and had been waiting there for hours. Apparently he'd been trying to contact Gwen's mother and hadn't been able to. Gwen checked her watch. "Dad said he'd call back every half hour, so I guess that means he'll call at seven."

"Twenty minutes. Plenty of time for a workout."

"Alec, I don't think—"

"Yes, you will. You'll spend the next twenty minutes stewing and fretting. Come on. Exercise is just what you need." He stood and held out his hand.

He was right and they both knew it.

Gwen allowed him to tug her toward the door.

"Okay, but I'm counting my walk over to your place as the warm-up."

Alec smiled down at her. "In that case, we're jogging."

During the past three days, Alec had rearranged the support beams on his exercise machine and had changed the order of the exercises. The whole process took closer to fifteen minutes than ten, but he was visibly pleased when they finished. Gwen would have liked to bask in his good mood—and he *had* offered dinner—but headed back to her apartment.

The phone started ringing right after she walked in the door, even though by her watch it was still a few minutes to seven.

"Gwen! Is everything all right?" Her father sounded nearly frantic.

"Dad, I work during the day and there's a two-hour time difference."

"Oh. Right. But that doesn't explain where your mother has been!"

Gwen fought a growing resentment. "Why do you care?" she asked quietly before she said worse.

"What kind of question is that?"

"You *left*. You didn't even say goodbye," she added.

"If I recall, *you* left that night without saying goodbye."

"It's not the same thing." And it wasn't. Not at all.

"Where's your mother?" he asked, sounding tired.

"I don't know."

"And this doesn't concern you?"

"She's probably out living her own life," Gwen said carefully. She could feel a wave of harsh words building and knew she was going to say something she shouldn't.

"I need to talk with her."

"Well, maybe she doesn't need to talk to you."

There was a heavy sigh. "Gwen, there are things here that you don't understand."

That did it. "No, *you* don't understand! And why should you? Mom has always catered to you, doing all the grunt work so you could become a big shot. Did you ever thank her? Did you ever even notice? Well, *I* noticed and I've gotta tell you, Dad, I am *not* going to repeat her mistake. I won't let myself." The last bit was more a reassurance to herself, Gwen acknowledged silently. Yeah, it was a struggle. She was dealing with it.

Her father was speaking in a tone Gwen had never heard him use. It reminded her of her boss, Mr. Eltzburg. "If you can be bothered to make sure your mother is safe, please do so. If either of you need to contact me, you may call the general store here and leave a message with either of the Bryces. They own the place."

Gwen stood by the phone for several minutes after hanging up. She hated to part from her father that way, but she was so frustrated by the whole situation she wanted to scream.

As it was, she yelped when there was a knock on the door. "Gwen? You okay?"

Alec was checking up on her. A male was showing concern. She sighed. It would help if he weren't so darn likable.

"No," she called.

"Let me in."

Gwen opened the door. "Men are clueless scum. You still want to come in?"

"Sure. It would be just the sort of clueless scummy thing you'd expect." He strode over to the sofa, tossed some papers on her coffee table, sat down in his usual spot—sprawling across two of the three cushions—and crossed his ankle over his knee. "What's up?"

It would serve him right if she told him. Maybe she would. "My parents are going to drive me nuts," she began and sat on the lone remaining cushion, as usual.

"Hang on a minute." He turned so that he was facing her, took her hand, then tilted his head slightly to the left. "Go on, Gwen. I'm here for you."

Gwen was a little rattled by Alec holding her hand. Okay, a lot rattled. What was that all about? And then she saw the ludicrously sympathetic expression he'd pasted on his features.

She narrowed her eyes. "What are you doing?"

"Listening attentively."

"You are not."

"I don't look sincere?"

Gwen snatched her hand away, ignoring the lingering warmth. "No."

Alec inhaled through his teeth then tried again. "How about now—does this look sincere?"

"You look like a used Bible salesman."

He ran a hand over his head. "I don't have the hair for it."

"Alec..."

"Hey, the article in *Scum Bag Quarterly* said that when a woman vents, a man is supposed to hold her hand, tilt his head and gaze into her eyes while occasionally murmuring 'hmm mmm.' You haven't given me the opportunity to murmur sympathetically yet."

"This isn't funny." And to her complete horror, Gwen felt a stinging at the edges of her eyes. She blinked rapidly, ready to bolt if she had to.

"Ah, Gwen."

The next thing she knew, Alec had leaned close enough to loop his arm around her shoulders and pull her toward him until her head was tucked just under his chin.

"Talk to me."

She felt the vibrations against her forehead. He was so solid and warm and made her feel so safe and secure and all those nonpolitically correct feelings independent women weren't supposed to feel.

And she talked, releasing all the pent-up words and frustrations. She even threw in a little about Eric, which was stupid, because no man wanted to hear rehashes of former relationships.

But Alec never said a word, he just gently kneaded her shoulder and rested his chin on the top of her head, letting her feel the steady thudding of his heart. At least she avoided crying.

Eventually she wound down. "You know, my mother and I always argued about the way she lived through Dad. I mean, I can't believe a woman who grew up during women's lib would actually go fifties retro, but she claimed she had a plan and I told her it was a stupid plan. I said this might happen, but I honestly never thought it would. I hate being right."

"Maybe you're not."

Gwen pushed out of Alec's arms ignoring the part of

her that wanted to stay. "How can you say that? My mother is here, deserted, and my father is clear across the country playing hermit."

"Gwen, they have a nearly thirty-year relationship. There are things that you can't know."

Her father had said essentially the same thing. "It still stinks. I'm not about to live my life for some man. He can live his life for me."

"Just so I understand your philosophy...you'd insist someone you love live the type of life you, yourself, despise? Interesting, Gwen."

"That's not it."

"Sounds like it to me. Would you really want the man in your life to be completely dependent on you in that way?"

Well, not when he put it like *that*.

"Or wouldn't you want him to be more of a man?".

Or that, either. Come to think of it, Alec was looking at her in a *very* manly way right now and she, well, she liked it. Especially since it was very easy to recall being held in his manly arms, tucked against his manly chest. And she wouldn't mind a little more manly tucking, actually—

The phone rang. Gwen had had enough of her father and decided not to answer it, especially since she and Alec were involved in something here, something she wanted to define before it ended—

"Gwen, it's Laurie." The noise in the background sounded as though she was at a party. "Look, I know it's none of my business, but if she were *my* mother, and a friend saw her, I'd want that friend to at least tell me about it—"

Oddly, it was Alec who beat her to the telephone. Gwen seemed frozen on the couch.

"Laurie, she's right here." He brought her the phone.

"Laurie?"

"Gwen, I'm at Fletchers. Your mom is here and she's, well, she's like...all these guys are hanging around her and she's..."

"*What?*"

"Well, I mean, she's flirting and buying rounds of drinks and, oh, hell, Gwen, I think she's going home with one of them."

Gwen now completely understood the saying about blood running cold. "Keep her from leaving. I'm on my way."

"But I don't know if I can get you in."

"I will get in if I have to break down the door." Shaken, Gwen barely got the phone back in the charger. "Mom's at Fletchers and she's gone nuts."

Scooping up his papers, Alec headed for the door. "Meet me in the parking lot."

"You're busy and—"

"These are just brochures. They can wait."

"Alec, you don't have to get involved."

The look he gave her was full of regally arrogant scorn. "You don't think much of me, do you?" And he was gone.

Gwen couldn't think of that now. Now, she had to find an outfit suitable for rescuing one's mother from a trendy club she'd managed to demonstrate enough trend to get into, while Gwen herself would certainly be turned away at the door. She just didn't have the clothes. Or couldn't get into the clothes. But she had shoes.

She threw on black silky pants, added her completely impractical Jimmy Choo shoes that would make her toes freeze, and unbuttoned an extra button on one of her blouses, ringed her eyes in black, and hoped they'd think she was going for the bohemian look.

Or the scared daughter who just climbed out of bed look.

She ran—hobbled—down the stairs, miraculously not rolling her ankle, and hurried toward her car.

Alec was already there, which was a good thing since she wouldn't have waited. Truly.

He wore a shirt and pants, but somehow, they were more than an ordinary shirt and pants. Maybe it was the parking lot lighting.

"Do you know where Fletchers is?" he asked, holding out his hand for the keys.

Gwen kept them and started the car. "Yes, I might not be on the A-list, but I do know about such things."

Alec said nothing, which irritated her because Gwen really, *really* wanted to pick an argument with someone and he was so available.

Staring straight ahead, she concentrated on the short drive. Richmond was just one street over, but she might have been in a different world. Clubs and restaurants lined both sides of the street and the everpresent traffic on one of the busiest stretches of freeway in Texas purred above them.

Fletchers, Gwen knew, was situated on the back part of a parking lot in a building marked only by a magenta-colored door and windows lined with lilac neon. Actually, a Tex-Mex fast-food place had been the previous tenant, and if Gwen remembered correctly, the lilac neon had been there then, too, though the door had been blue. Apparently, people, even trendy people who should have given it a chance, didn't accept that color scheme and Tex-Mex.

The place was crowded. Too crowded. Valet parking was Gwen's only option. Determinedly, she drove under the covered walkway and waited for one of the "hosts" standing outside to amble over.

They took their own sweet time about approaching her car. Under ordinary circumstances, Gwen would have been intimidated, but these weren't ordinary circumstances. She gave the hulk with the suit that had obviously been tailored to go over some serious muscles—no ten-minute workouts for him—a direct look and arched her eyebrow ever so slightly.

It was enough to bring him to her car. "May I help you, ma'am?"

"Are you the valet?" she asked and tried to open her car door. She couldn't because he was leaning against it.

"Ma'am, this is a private party."

"It is not. It is Fletchers and I'm going in."

Ever so slightly, the man shook his head.

"My mother is already inside."

A flicker of expression crossed his face—uncertainty?—and Gwen guessed that she'd surprised him, something that probably didn't happen often.

"How're you doing, Devon?" Alec asked quietly beside her. He put the accent on the second syllable of the man's name.

The man ducked until he could see inside the car. His gaze flicked over Gwen and alighted on Alec. "Mr. Fleming. Welcome, sir."

Hulk had the door open so fast, Gwen nearly fell out onto the asphalt. Nevertheless, she swung out her legs, noticed Hulk—no De*von*—noticing her shoes and marveled over the subtle change in his demeanor as he helped her out of the car.

"Devon, this is Ms. Kempner," Alec informed the man as he came around the side of the car.

Gwen noticed that Alec passed the man a folded bill, but pretended not to.

"What is your drink, Ms. Kempner?" Devon asked as he waved away the valet and slid into the driver's seat himself. The entire car tilted to one side.

Oh, great, a drink test. She gave an elaborate sigh. "I'm still stuck on Cosmopolitans." She figured the once-trendy drink was now passé, but didn't know the current drink of the moment.

Devon gave her a slight nod and drove off with her car.

Alec, hands shoved in his pockets tilted his head and peered at her shoes. "May I say that those are *excellent* shoes?"

Gwen knew they were excellent shoes, but she didn't know men noticed. Now two had in one evening. She should start saving up for another pair immediately. "Tell me, Alec, not that I'm not grateful, you understand, but how is it that a poor, struggling entrepreneur is recognized by the bouncer at Fletchers?"

"Because before the owners started Fletchers, they had another word-of-mouth club called Pews, which was in an old church. Before that, there was Michelangelos—spare and arty. Before that, they were 88—a piano bar. Before that—"

"Got it."

"And I wouldn't refer to Devon as a bouncer."

"Well, what is he?"

"Someone you want on your side."

Gwen nodded, thinking that with Devon on her side, there wouldn't be a whole lot of room for her.

They neared the door, which swung inward when they approached. Inside, a hostess in a black-light illuminated booth drew design squiggles on plastic strips with fluorescent pens, then attached the strips to their wrists. Gwen's was green—an appropriate color choice for the evening—and Alec's was blue with a pink mouth print from the hostess's glowing lipstick. After they'd been tagged, they walked through an archway and were met by a waitress holding a tray with two drinks on it. One glass held an amber-colored liquid and the other was a martini glass with a pinkish liquid. That would be her Cosmopolitan. Nice touch.

"Devon invites you to be his guests for the evening," the waitress said.

"Express our appreciation to Devon." Alec smiled and deftly slipped her another of his folded bills.

Gwen would have felt guiltier about him spending money—and she knew better than to offer to reimburse him—if she hadn't been searing her taste buds with her drink. Not being a martini fan, she'd never actually consumed a Cosmopolitan. And it looked like she never would. Still, it made a pretty prop as she scanned the dimly lit room.

"Is your drink all right?" Alec asked.

"It tastes just the way it's supposed to."

"But you don't like it."

"Ugh," she admitted and made a face.

"Here. I'll get you another—"

"No! I mean, I'll just hold it awhile. It goes with my outfit."

He grinned at her, the lighting making his teeth unnaturally white. Throughout the room, pools of black light picked up the fluorescent wristbands of the patrons who, for the most part, were listening to a three-piece combo playing new arrangements of old swing music.

"Oh, good, you're here." Laurie and Brian appeared. Laurie looked over Gwen's shoulder. "Hey, and you actually got him in. Way to go."

"He got *me* in," Gwen corrected her. It was only fair.

"Did he?" Laurie studied Alec as he and Brian shook hands, then turned Gwen toward the bar. "There she is."

Just as she spoke a woman's laughter rang out with unmistakable familiarity, though Gwen didn't recall her mother ever being so *loud* before. But, yes, there was Suzanne, legs crossed, perched on a barstool. She was surrounded by men Gwen's age.

And she was wearing The Skirt.

9

ALEC WAS GLAD he'd tipped Devon fifty bucks and he didn't begrudge the waitress the twenty, either. Now, if Gwen had to come back here, she shouldn't have any trouble.

The fact that he'd just blown the deposit for the brochures he was going to have printed didn't bother him at all. Gwen wasn't an "after" picture yet, anyway. And if it hadn't been for her and her party leftovers, he wouldn't have been able to save the money out of his food budget.

Still, he marveled at just how unconcerned he was at greasing the wheels at Fletchers on her behalf.

He savored a long swallow of his bourbon and branch and felt it warm a path to his stomach. Good stuff. He hadn't had any good stuff in months. In fact, other than the odd beer here and there—New Year's Eve excepted—he hadn't had stuff at all.

And yes, he did enjoy it more now. He never thought he'd lived a particularly indulgent life, but he had noticed how it had taken more and more to satisfy him. Peeling away all the flash and razzle-dazzle made him value the basics more and look for those basics in others.

Gwen was loaded with basics. Unfortunately, she

wanted the razzle-dazzle. He watched her grimace and try to drink her Cosmopolitan.

"Is your drink all right?"

"It tastes just the way it's supposed to," she said.

He could tell she didn't like it and offered to order a different one, but she refused. He knew she wasn't going to drink any more of it and at that moment he knew Gwen could handle all the razzle-dazzle life threw at her because it would never be the be-all and end-all for her.

He stared at her as she searched the room, seeing her in a different way, though that could just be the weird lighting.

But in case it wasn't, he took another swallow of his drink. He'd had, he suspected, a profound realization and it left him shaken, which in itself was something to consider. Because if profound thoughts shook him, then he had some serious character development ahead of him.

Fortunately, Gwen's friend found her just then and pointed out Gwen's mother, who, Alec thought, was looking mighty fine. *Mighty* fine. There was no way he'd ever tell Gwen, or if she asked, he'd attribute it to the distance. And the lighting. And a pair of very nice legs Gwen had inherited—*not* that it was likely Gwen was going to ask, especially since she was headed straight for her mother and had clearly forgotten all about him.

He drained his drink before following after her and another miraculously appeared at his elbow. He started to refuse, then thought what the hell? He wasn't driving and it looked like it was going to be one of those nights.

Gwen cut right through the phalanx of men until she was at her mother's side.

"Gwen! What are you doing here?"

Gwen drew a deep breath. Alec groaned inwardly, but to his relief Gwen hoisted herself on a newly vacated bar stool. "Just hanging." She gave her mother a cool look and brought her drink to her lips.

Alec was relieved that she wasn't the scene type. He pushed his way closer with more difficulty than Gwen. Her mother noticed him.

"And who is this good-looking guy? Hi, I'm Suze."

"*Suze?*"

Her mother gave her a look.

"Uh, that's Alec. He's—"

"I'm Gwen's date," he inserted, finding he wanted all the males in the vicinity to be absolutely clear on that point. Why he wanted them to be clear on that point, he wasn't prepared to explore just at the moment.

"Gwen!" Her mother shook his hand and arched her eyebrow at Gwen, which, okay, he'd admit it, gave his ego a little buzz.

"And now, I want you to meet my friends." Gwen's mother cast a beaming look at her admirers. "This is Antonio," she grasped the arm of the young guy next to her. "And Jason, and Travis, and Rob, and Dirk, and Colt, and Matthew, and CJ, and...Lorenzo." She purred the last name and leaned toward him smiling.

Alec considered himself a man of scruples, which excluded things like staring down the blouse of his date's mother. However, Lorenzo was not dating Gwen, therefore, he had no such scruples. Or something like that. The point was, he made no secret of looking.

Gwen seemed like she was about to be sick.

Alec leaned close to her—and speaking of blouses... but, alas, they were not—and whispered next to her ear, "Let's dance."

"Are you insane?"

"Regroup."

Abandoning her drink, Gwen allowed him to pull her away from her mother. When they cleared the group, it closed again.

Gwen stared backward until they reached the dance floor. "Alec, what am I going to do?" she wailed as he pulled her into his arms.

"Maybe you won't have to do anything."

"Oh, come on! She's flaunting herself at men who are wearing more than one gold chain at a time!"

At that moment, the band struck up a salsa number and laughter sounded from the group. Gwen's mother headed for the dance floor with two of her chain-clad admirers.

Gwen was oblivious to the change in music and continued to stay in his arms—which was perfectly fine with him—and sway as her mother... Well. The woman could dance, Alec had to admit. Yes. She was dancing, all right. Sure was. If one could call those movements dancing. He looked longingly down at Gwen, but her attention was wholly fixed on her gyrating mother and the men who gyrated with her. Or more accurately, against her.

In fact, Gwen demonstrated a lot of potential

strength in her arms, judging by her grip on his shoulder.

"Alec...*do* something. She won't listen to me, I know it."

Alec knew better, but uttered the fateful words anyway. "What do you want me to do?"

"Keep those guys away from her."

"What? You want me to cut in?"

"Would you?"

And—and do *that* with her *mother?* "Oh, no. I—"

"*Please.*" Gwen looked up at him as though he were a knight on a white charger.

"Gwen..." Bad idea. Bad, bad idea.

She backed off the dance floor.

Okay. Fine. Just *fine.* Alec started toward her mother knowing that this was one of those no-win situations that women were so talented at concocting.

On the plus side, he danced a mean salsa.

GWEN WAS HAVING an out-of-body-experience and when it was all over, she hoped she landed in someone else's body. Preferably—no, she would insist on it—someone who could wear that skirt.

It had to be the skirt. It had to be.

How else could she explain the vision of her mother dancing the salsa, with multiple partners, in the middle of a postage stamp size dance floor in one of the hottest clubs in Houston?

Gwen stared. She even absently sipped at the foul drink and waved away the next round. "I'm driving." Seconds later a fizzy fruit thing appeared.

She drank three of those.

Alec was holding his own with Antonio and Lorenzo and other assorted chained men.

Okay. Alec was more than holding his own, though she wished he wouldn't do that move where he lifted both his hands over her mother's head as she bent backward.

After awhile, Gwen just stared at the rippling skirt. She could swear that it was taunting her.

Look what I can do it seemed to say.

At first, Gwen thought she could see through it, but with the light in here, she wasn't sure. Then she decided it was just the mesmerizing, but subtle shimmer of the fabric and the way it clung and released depending on the movements of the dance.

People were watching. No. *Couples* were watching. Gwen was alone.

Not one man had hit on her. She crossed her legs and swung her foot so any interested parties could check out her sexy shoes.

All parties were only interested in the floor show.

Little did they know that the real show was just a few feet off the dance floor, where a lone woman in silky black pants and Jimmy Choo shoes was having a life-altering realization.

And Gwen's realization was that she no longer was interested in becoming successful all on her own. No, she wanted to become successfully attached.

And the person she wanted to become attached to was Alec.

Unfortunately, he was currently attached to her mother. Yes, he'd done exactly as she'd asked him to do—emerged triumphant over all the dark-haired, dark-eyed, swivel-hipped, multichained lotharios.

Yes, Alec had outswiveled them all. And enjoyed it, too, judging by his intent dark-eyed gaze and white-toothed smile. With every fiber of her being, Gwen wanted him to look at *her* that way.

Between the expression on Alec's face and the movements of the dance, Gwen's mouth went dry and she knocked back her drink. Another magically appeared within moments. She really ought to tip that poor girl.

And she ought to lay off the juice, loaded with calories as it was. Because right then and there, Gwen vowed that she was going to get into the skirt. Look what it was doing for her mother!

And speaking of her mother...eventually Gwen would have to deal with the fact that her mother seemed not at all troubled that Alec was Gwen's date—but she'd save that for another life-altering moment.

"ARE YOU FOLLOWING ME?" Alec asked her later. Much, much later—2:00 a.m. to be precise. Or precise might be 2:11 a.m., but it wasn't necessary to be *that* precise. Suffice it to say, it was late when they finally left Fletchers after seeing that her mother got into her car—alone.

"Yes, I am following you," Gwen answered him. Conversation had been thin on the way home.

"Why?"

"Because you have the key."

"Yes, to *my* apartment. Your apartment is in the other direction."

"I know."

"Gwen...I'm beat."

"I imagine you are, what with all that exercise. The only exercise I got was walking to the ladies' room after drinking all those fruit thingies."

Alec was silent for a moment. They reached the bottom of the stairs and he turned to face her. "Gwen, you asked me to intervene with your mother. You saw what I was up against."

"Yes. My mother. Frequently." She started up the stairs.

"Can't this wait?" he called, sounding unutterably weary.

"No."

He muttered something Gwen was pretty sure she wasn't meant to hear. Bounding up the stairs, though where he found the energy to do so, she couldn't imagine, he pounded once on the door, then unlocked it. With an exaggerated bow, he gestured for her to go inside. As she did so, a gray streak disappeared into the bedroom.

Gwen went straight to the exercise machine, sat down, took off her shoes, and began the routine.

Alec went to shut the bedroom door. "What are you doing?"

"Exercising."

"In the middle of the night?"

"It's past the middle. I need to unwind." Gwen jerked her protesting arms together. Tough. They were going to have to get with the program.

Alec watched her, leaning over to correct her position when she changed exercises. He smelled like cigarette smoke and somebody who'd been dancing the salsa with somebody else's mother.

Gwen threw in a couple of extra reps, then started on her legs.

Alec gave her a brooding look. "I'm going to regret this, but tell me what's bothering you."

"I want a key to your apartment." She surprised both of them with that.

"Why?"

"So I can get in here to exercise when I want to."

His face didn't change expressions. "Can you remember to knock on the door to warn the cat first?"

Gwen nodded and repositioned her knees.

"I'll have one made."

No arguing? He was actually going to give her a key? Gwen looked up at him. He looked right back. It was a serious look. "Now tell me what this is all about."

She didn't have to tell him. She shouldn't tell him. Pointing out this evening's humiliation wouldn't enhance her attractiveness, on the minuscule chance he hadn't noticed.

But. But he'd just agreed to give her a key with nothing more than a warning about the cat.

Gwen sighed. "My mother."

"Argh!" Alec turned to the wall and beat his head against it a couple of times. "I knew it."

"No! I don't blame you."

"What did you say? I was busy pounding sense into my head."

"Thanks for keeping those men away from my mother."

"You're welcome." He nodded at her. "You've spent enough time on the leg presses."

Gwen continued. "So I'll do extra."

"How much extra?" he asked carefully.

"Triple sessions, at least."

"You'll wear yourself out."

"Good!"

"But you're only supposed to be doing ten minutes. You'll progress too quickly and my chart will be all wrong."

"I can't wait for your chart," she snarled.

Shaking his head, Alec sat down on the seat and effectively stopped her.

"Move."

"Nope." He wore a patient smile.

"I need to exercise," she grumbled.

He didn't say anything. He didn't move, either.

Gwen stared at the shirt button in the middle of his chest. "I have to do *something*. You can't possibly know how humiliating it was to sit there—alone—while men swarmed around my mother. I mean, sure, I'm not looking for a relationship right now, but it would be nice to at least be noticed."

He lifted her chin with his finger. "You were noticed, but you give off a strong 'unavailable' signal."

"I do not! Besides, I wore the shoes."

"Yes, but you wore them with pants."

"Well...my mother had my skirt!" Reminded that she still couldn't fit in the skirt, Gwen grabbed the overhead bar. If Alec didn't move, she'd bean him with it.

He tilted back as she brought it down, then reached for her hands and straightened her wrists. "You also ignore signals men give you."

"Trust me, *nobody* was signaling me tonight."

Alec gave her a funny look. "You sure about that?" Looking into her eyes, he reached behind her and pressed a fist against her spine. "Sit up straight." Gwen straightened, bringing her closer to him, since he didn't move.

His eyes were very dark and his body was very warm. Or that might have been her body. Or both bodies. Gwen swayed toward him ever so slightly.

"You're arching your back."

Honestly, couldn't he be the least bit affected? "Make up your mind."

"I have." He splayed his hand across her stomach. "Tighten and breathe out."

Gwen turned her head so she wouldn't breathe in his face.

"I may have been responsible for cutting down on the traffic to your table."

"How?"

"I let them know you were with me."

"You did?"

"Uh-huh."

"How?"

"Eye contact, mostly."

"What, are you saying men are telepathic?"

"I'm saying that there's protocol." Moving his hands, he placed them over her biceps. "Pull."

It felt strange to pull the bar with Alec's hands on her arms. Strange and kind of sensual. It was, without a doubt, the best set of reps ever. "And you sent a 'hands off, guys' signal around the room?"

"Something like that."

"And it was so strong that even when you were out there dancing with my mother and I was alone at the table, they honored it?"

"You didn't trump the signal." He took the bar from her. "Let me see how much weight you're pulling." Positioning himself, straight back, sucked in stomach and all that, Alec pulled the bar down to his shoulders and raised it again. She could see the muscles beneath his shirt. Alec had nice muscles.

"What would I have had to do to trump the signal?"

Alec raised and lowered the bar before answering. Gwen knew she was supposed to be concentrating on form and she was, actually. It just happened to be Alec's form.

"Eye contact and body language, mostly." He released the bar, stood and made some sort of adjustment with his fingers. Gwen tried not to notice that his waist was about level with her line of sight.

"Oh, like this?" She winked and gave an "over here, fellas" sort of wave.

Alec's lips curved, but he didn't quite smile. "Try that." He straddled the bench and faced her again.

Gwen pulled on the bar. "Ow!"

"Better workout?" He put his hand on her bicep, moving his thumb across her arm.

"Do you feel that? It's like a rock. You're going to turn me into Mr. Universe." She abandoned the bar. Her arms didn't have to fit into the skirt, anyway.

"Sore?"

"Yes," she admitted.

Alec started massaging her arm, kneading her sore

muscles. "This evening, you were watching your mother."

She'd been watching him just as much, but wasn't going to correct him.

"You weren't interested in being approached and it showed."

She extended her other arm and he went to work on it. He had good hands. Steady and slow. Rhythmical. "There were men on the dance floor, too. I could have been watching them."

"Did you make eye contact?"

"How could I? They were drooling over my mother!"

Alec released her arm and stood. "You know, Gwen, you wouldn't recognize a signal from a man if it bit you on the nose."

She stood, too. "Just because I don't pump up every stray ego that floats by doesn't mean I don't recognize when a man is interested, and I'm telling you, not one man paid any attention to me tonight."

"Really." He blinked, then glanced toward the bedroom door. "I'm heading for bed...care to join me?"

"Oh, ha ha." Gwen picked up her purse and walked across the room. "Good night, Alec. And thanks."

"Sure." He approached the door. Hand on the knob, he looked down at her. And for the briefest of moments, something in his expression made Gwen think he was actually going to kiss her good-night.

But he only pulled open the door. "Good night, Gwen."

10

ALEC STARED morosely over the top of his computer monitor at the exercising Gwen. That was one focused woman. Too bad she was so focused that she was missing some interesting opportunities for exercise of another type.

The total irony of his situation wasn't lost on Alec. He, who had spent the past six months living for his fledgling business, was being ignored by a woman who was concentrating on her career.

Well, no, not ignored, exactly. Just keeping things status quo. Only Alec wanted to change the status quo. He hadn't decided exactly how, but he sort of thought he and Gwen could improvise as they went along.

Gwen wasn't going along. Gwen had ignored all signs of Alec's interest in her. To be fair—and he wanted to be fair because it was more flattering to him—he'd pretty much treated her as he always had, so how was she supposed to know he wasn't thinking of her as he always had? It wasn't like she was *rejecting* him, or anything. No, it wasn't anything like that in spite of his *intense* and prolonged signaling of four nights ago.

He was just going to have to transmit his signals on a different frequency.

"I know if I can come up with a fabulous suggestion, they'll see I'm ready for a promotion."

And louder. Possibly louder.

Gwen had been babbling all during her exercise session—her second of the day. And if she followed her latest schedule, she'd show up again about nine o'clock tonight.

He'd given her a key to his apartment—talk about a signal—but so far, he'd been here each time she'd wanted to exercise so she hadn't had to use it.

"The designer coffee craze has cut into Kwik Koffee's sales. The thing is," Gwen paused and peeled off her T-shirt, revealing a black sports bra over unblemished white skin, then grabbed the arm bar.

Gwen had really excellent skin. Alec swallowed a whimper.

"The thing is," she continued, "our coffee is just as good as theirs and blind tastings prove that people can't consistently tell the difference between ours and the ritzy coffee house coffees, so upgrading isn't going to help."

"Perception is everything." Alec was pleased that he could speak in a normal voice.

"I know, but a heavy advertising campaign would result in higher costs being passed on to the consumer." Gwen stood to reverse her seating on the bench.

Alec held out a doomed hope that she'd pull off the baggy shorts and finish exercising in the bicycle ones she wore beneath. She didn't.

"You know, we've got the same problem at our company," he said. "Brand names are leaching sales from the house brand. People are willing to pay more just to buy the same names they see in the grocery store."

"So start selling in the grocery store," Gwen said.

They'd tried. "Talk about competitive. Have you researched what it takes to get a shelf space commitment?"

"No." She stared off into the distance, her arms hanging seductively over the padded bar as she squeezed her thighs together.

Alec stared at the brochure layouts on his computer monitor. Of course he didn't *see* the layouts. He saw Gwen squeezing and pulsing and throbbing and sweating and...and he could hear her breathing. Heavily. And every once in a while she made a tiny moan that sounded *exactly* like—

"Kiosks!"

"Gesundheit."

"Alec!" Laughing she gathered her hair back from her face and refastened her ponytail. Doing so revealed considerably more of her stomach, but Alec wasn't going to tell her.

"What do you think of freestanding coffee kiosks in malls and even on street corners downtown? Maybe even movie theater lobbies. It would both advertise *and* bring in money. It would make people more familiar with our coffee because we'd sell it cheaper than the coffeehouses. We've got too many dispensing machines in inventory and this would be a way to use them...I wonder what it costs to rent floor space in the mall walkways?"

"A lot." Why had he never noticed just how sexy a

woman looked when she talked business while she exercised?

"It can't be too much or there wouldn't be so many carts selling cheap silver jewelry."

Alec opened his mouth, but whatever he'd been going to say escaped without being said and was replaced with, surprisingly *not* Gwen, but visions of kiosks selling Fleming Snack Foods.

Or kiosks selling snack foods *and* coffee.

He liked it. He liked it a lot.

Quickly, he opened a new file on his computer and started typing in everything he could think of. He hadn't been working at the company for months and wasn't sure where they were in terms of expansion, but Gwen had brought up a problem they'd encountered. And her solution was worth checking out.

"Hellllooooo. Alec!"

He glanced up.

"I'm leaving now."

He nodded at her and went back to work.

GWEN TRUDGED back to her apartment. If she exercised naked, Alec wouldn't notice. The past several days, he'd barely bothered to check to see if she was using the correct form.

Oh, well. There was always the skirt. She'd wrestled it back from her mother and it hung in the closet waiting for her to put it on.

Gwen resolutely fixed herself a lettuce salad with fat-free dressing and called her mother, so she wouldn't be tempted to eat any more. She was rarely hungry after talking with her mother these days.

Her mother actually answered the phone. "You're home!" Gwen said around a mouthful of lettuce.

"Yes." Suzanne sighed. "Fletchers hasn't been as much fun the last couple of nights. I don't suppose you'd like to bring Alec—"

"No." Gwen chewed and swallowed. "You know, Mom, doesn't it bother you even a little bit that he was my date?" Suzanne didn't know the true circumstances and she didn't need to.

"Of course not. You made him dance with me to keep those other men away."

Gwen nearly choked. "Did he tell you that?" How could he?

"He didn't have to. And I was touched that you wanted to protect me, but truly, Gwen, it isn't necessary. Though, honey, I wouldn't have missed that dance for *anything*."

"Have you heard from Dad?" Gwen asked pointedly. At this rate, she'd wouldn't even finish her salad.

"Not directly. He's left a message, so I left one for him with the people at the store telling him I was fine. And busy. I made it a point to tell him I was busy."

Time for a change of subject. Gwen told her mother about her kiosk plan and to her surprise, her mother had some good ideas. Actually her mother had a lot of *great* ideas, so great, that Gwen grabbed some paper and pencil and took notes. "Mom, you're good at this."

"Politicking for ideas is what I've done for years. I'll check my Rolodex and give you some names. Maybe I'll make a couple of calls."

"Well, you don't have to do that."

"I'd be happy to."

Gwen hung up shortly afterward feeling a little nervous about getting her mother involved. But at least she was home instead of clubbing. Keeping her there would be worth any embarrassment.

On Friday, one week and about thirty exercise sessions after the Fletchers fiasco, Gwen was ready for ice cream. Really ready. So ready that she bought a pint of her favorite Chocolate Rapids with fudge, nuts, caramel, marshmallow and chocolate chunks.

She practically broke a nail tearing into it. She dug in a spoon and brought an obscene hunk right up to her lips—and stopped. She could feel the cold. She could smell the chocolate.

And she put it down.

Had she made *any* progress with the skirt?

Gwen stared at her ice cream. She *wanted* ice cream. She *needed* ice cream. Her willpower was fading.

Gwen forced herself into the bedroom and removed the skirt from the hanger.

The last time she'd tried it on, the zipper needed another two and a half inches to close. Maybe by now, she could move it up another inch. She wasn't wearing control-top panty hose, so she didn't hold out hope for more than that. But even a little progress would give her the strength to put the ice cream back into the freezer.

Slowly she took off the pants she had on, which actually were looser than she remembered.

Skirt time. Gwen stepped into it, enjoying the silky feel as it skimmed over her legs. It was great fabric. Carefully, she eased it up over her hips.

That wasn't too bad. Next, the zipper.

Gwen sucked in her stomach and tugged gently. Tugged some more. And more.

Surprised, she looked down and watched as the zipper made it all the way to the waistband and stopped. And it only stopped because there was no more zipper to zip. Before it could change its mind, Gwen fastened the hook.

But, of course she wasn't actually *breathing* and she couldn't go around with a sucked in stomach all night. Still...Gwen took an experimental breath.

The skirt held.

Gradually, she relaxed her stomach muscles.

And the skirt held. Held nicely, thank you very much.

She was wearing the skirt! Gwen looked at herself in the full-length mirror and added the Jimmy Choo shoes.

Okay. Next, she searched for an appropriate top and found a red fuzzy one that she'd always felt was a little too tight and a little too low-cut and a little too red and attracted a little too much attention.

It was still too red and too low-cut and tight, but she didn't care. She looked hot.

She had to show Alec. Without giving herself time to think about it, Gwen shoved the ice cream back into the freezer, got his key and headed over to his apartment.

"ALEC? ARE YOU HOME?"

She was early, but Alec didn't care. He had looked up some figures on her kiosk idea and wanted to talk to her. He also had an idea he wanted to run past her.

"Come on in," he called. He went over to his exercise machine to pull it out from the wall and set it up for her, when the door opened.

"Ta-da!" A beaming Gwen bounced into the room. "Look!"

Alec's mouth went dry. "Gwen?"

She twirled around. "How's this for results?"

He swallowed, or tried to. He was suddenly only interested in one figure—hers. "You look..." He trailed off with a gesture. "Red." Deep within him, a tremor began. He was very much afraid it was his inner caveman awakening.

Her face fell. "Too red?"

"No." He shook his head.

She pulled at her sweater. "Too tight? Do I look slutty?"

"No." His voice had risen an octave. He cleared his throat. "No. You look very tasty—*tasteful*."

"Well, *tasteful* wasn't quite the look I was going for, but with this V-neck, I figured the WonderBra would be overkill." She pushed her arms together and manufactured an impressive cleavage. "I don't know—what do you think? To cleave, or not to cleave?"

Think? She expected him to think? "Uhhhh..."

"Yeah, you're right." She released her breasts and gestured to her skirt. "So, how about the skirt?"

With difficulty, Alec transferred his gaze to the black skirt she was wearing. It was just a skirt and not particularly short or tight...except that it did cling ever so nicely. He peered closer. Was it see-through or was he just imagining her legs?

The more he stared, the better it looked. The better *she* looked.

"Come on, Alec, I feel like partying! Take me to Fletchers. Please?"

"Now?"

"Of course, now!"

Alec looked at her beaming face above the most perfect red sweater ever knit, paired with a skirt that lovingly caressed her legs, and a pair of impossibly high-heeled shoes that did strange and wonderful things to her walk.

He was in such trouble.

ALEC NURSED his third complimentary designated-driver drink and stared at the dance floor where Gwen, who claimed not to know how to salsa, had proved to be a fast and gifted student.

Too bad he hadn't been the teacher.

As soon as they'd walked into Fletchers, Alec had draped an arm around her shoulders and had warned away any stray dogs with his usual, "Hey, buddy, she's with me," look. And in return, all he'd gotten was, "Yeah, right. Keep her if you can," expressions.

Never had the great men's collective so quickly turned on one of its own.

And Gwen didn't seem to notice. She was surrounded by men with whom she'd flirted, danced and teased. She...she was *glowing*. Alec didn't want her glowing for anybody but him.

The ultimate, the absolute ultimate was when Devon *returned* Alec's tip and danced with Gwen during his break.

After that, Gwen had all the men in the place to herself. Judging by the empty tables, the women's bathroom was jammed with pouting females.

Alec felt like joining them.

Just then, Gwen's partner bent her backward in a whiplash until her hair brushed the floor. And that was another thing—who'd taught her to fling her hair around like that? Did she know the effect it had? Did she?

Gwen's current partner—one of the multichained men she'd scorned last week—did a series of crossover breaks and then a huge throwout turn.

Gwen twirled and was jerked back close enough so that she bounced off the guy's chest. He immediately pulled her close against him. The music ended with a crashing flourish. They froze, looking like a tequila commercial, then he bent his head.

Alec shot out of his chair and stormed across the dance floor. If anybody was going to be pulling Gwen close, it was going to be Alec.

"Thanks for dancing with my date, buddy. Now I'm going to show you how it's done." He pulled Gwen close, close enough to make him glad that Gwen-all-Gwen was next to him and not the WonderBra.

She gave him a look that she had no business giving.

And he gave her one right back.

Then they began to dance.

GWEN KEPT TELLING herself that if her mother could do it, then it must be all right, but Alec was dancing so *very* close and she was enjoying it so *very* much, that she was pretty sure they were doing something illegal.

This skirt was something else. Never again would

she doubt its power. She broke away from the intense eye contact with Alec and surveyed the room with satisfaction. Every man here had noticed her.

Alec had finally noticed her.

All hail the power of the mighty skirt.

Alec pulled her into a side-by-side "cuddle" position just as the music ended and bent his head to her ear. "I'm taking you home. Now."

He was jealous—actually jealous! This was so much better than just being noticed.

She rubbed her hip against him. "I love it when you go all strong and manly."

His strong and manly arm tensed around her and he maneuvered them through the crowd. Gwen waved at all her new—male—friends. Oddly, not one of them moved to intercept Alec.

Devon apparently got word of their imminent departure, because just as they made their way outside, he was driving Gwen's car from the far reaches of the parking lot.

"'Bye, Devon!" She wiggled her fingers at him.

He glanced at Alec before smiling faintly.

This was way too much fun.

Alec had elected himself driver for the evening and started the car.

"That was soooooo fabulous." Gwen scooted over until she was right next to him.

"Put on your seat belt, Gwen," he said through clenched teeth.

"But it's all the way over there!"

He stopped at the parking lot entrance, reached

across her for the shoulder strap and pulled it into place.

"But Alec, you didn't want me so far away when we were dancing."

"It's safer this way."

She was being mean, but darn it, he'd taken her for granted for such a long time. "Whew! I'm so hot." Raising her hair off her neck, she fanned herself with her hand, then pulled out her sweater and blew down the neckline.

The car jerked to a stop after Alec nearly ran a red light.

This was just too easy. Slipping off her shoe, she reached for her foot and massaged her toes, knowing that the skirt had slid up her thighs. Well, it wasn't like he hadn't seen her thighs before. He'd measured them, for pity's sake!

Alec said nothing, but she could hear him taking long, deep breaths.

For some reason, thighs showing because a skirt had ridden up were better than thighs revealed by a pair of shorts. Go figure.

"Mmm," she moaned. "That feels sooo gooood."

Alec peeled the car around the corner so fast Gwen had to abandon her foot to brace herself against the door.

"Took that corner a little fast," he mumbled, looking frazzled as he turned into their apartment complex.

Frazzled looked cute on him.

"Alec?"

"Hmm?"

"Thanks for taking me to Fletchers tonight."

"Hmm."

"I enjoyed our dance, too."

"Hmm-mmm."

He parked the car, claiming her rightful spot so she didn't have to walk as far, which was good, because these shoes weren't made for walking.

"Did you enjoy our dance?" she prompted.

"Yes." Before opening the door, he shot her a look that told her she'd gone as far as she'd better go without being able to back it up.

And the thought of backing it up was, well, tempting. But while she sat in her car and thought about it, Alec was leaving.

"Good night, Gwen. See you tomorrow." He took off.

Wasn't he even going to walk her to her apartment? Gwen took pity on him. Gathering her shoes, she got out of the car and ran after him. "Alec!"

"Good night, Gwen," he called over his shoulder.

He was angry and she could hardly blame him. All this time, she'd just been Gwen, his neighbor, and tonight, she'd used the skirt on him. She'd changed the rules without warning him. It wasn't fair.

"Alec, wait! I've got something to tell you."

He slowed, but he didn't stop and he didn't turn around.

"Alec, I'm sorry!"

He stopped, hand on the stair railing, but didn't look at her. "For what?"

Gwen limped up to him. "For wearing the skirt in front of you."

"*What* are you talking about?"

She gestured down at herself. "This, well, this isn't an ordinary skirt. It's got special powers."

The look he gave her was not encouraging. "Good night, Gwen," he said for the third time and climbed the stairs.

She climbed after him. "Alec, I'm serious! It attracts men. You didn't have a chance."

"You're scaring me." He unlocked the door, forgetting to bang on it first. A gray blur streaked between his legs. "That damn cat!" Alec sucked the breath between his teeth.

"I'll get him." Gwen leaned over the railing. "Armageddon, get your tail in here right now, or you spend the night outside!"

"Like that'll scare him."

There was a yowl from the shadows beneath the stairs. "Go inside, Alec," Gwen instructed him. She bent down. "Come on, Army. It's okay."

Muttering, Alec stomped inside his apartment.

"He's gone. Come on, kitty." Gwen stepped inside the apartment and let the light shine out. "I'm going to close the door," she called. Inch by inch, she reduced the light. "Hurry up, Armageddon..."

At the last possible moment, the cat squeezed through and ran for the bedroom.

Gwen shut the door. "There." She turned, expecting thanks, but Alec only glared at her from across the room as he unbuttoned his cuffs.

"About the skirt, I—I'd rather not go into the reasons *why* I wore it in front of you, but I apologize for doing so."

He said nothing, only began unbuttoning his shirt.

"Say something!"

"Why the skirt and not the top?"

"Huh?"

"If you're going to apologize for something, apologize for wearing that sweater thing."

"But there's nothing special about the sweater."

He snorted.

"It's the skirt that has the powers." Quickly Gwen told him all about Torrie, then Chelsea, and now her.

He'd finished unbuttoning his shirt and it hung open as he stood, hands on his hips and listened to her story in an irritated disbelief.

Gwen wondered if he knew that the black shirt looked really good against his chest. And that tanned muscles were impressive and all that, but she was a chest hair kind of gal. And a low-slung pants kind of gal, too. "So you see, it's okay that you felt conflicted and confused." *Lord knows I feel conflicted and confused.*

"Conflicted, yes. But confused? Not a chance."

"But it's true. I only look good to you because the skirt's a man magnet. And so you're…attracted."

Alec stared at her. She really, really wished she knew what was going through his mind.

"If that's what you think," he drawled, "then take the skirt off."

11

Okay, MAYBE Gwen *didn't* want to know what was going through his mind.

Alec stared at her from across the room, his chest rising and falling. She knew because she was staring at his chest, waiting for him to crack one of his Alec smiles and call her chicken, or quote Scooby-Doo dialogue or something else to break the tension.

They hadn't watched Scooby-Doo cartoons in, oh, ages. They were probably due for a popcorn marath—

"In case you didn't get it, that was a signal."

Gwen slowly dragged her gaze away from Alec's chest to his face.

No Alec smile. No Scooby dialogue. Lots of tension.

Yeah, that was a signal, all right. A strong signal.

So what was she going to do about it?

Gwen swallowed. Her palms were damp and she smoothed them against her thighs. As she did so, she'd swear the skirt quivered. The fabric was warm to the touch, but that was just because she'd raced up the stairs. Right?

What are you afraid of? That if you take the skirt off, Alec won't find you attractive—or that he will?

She had to know. It was crazy that she even considered that the whole skirt story might be true...but she had to know.

Alec was waiting, staring intently at her from across the room.

She had to break the spell—and if the sight of her pasty white thighs weren't enough to put a man off, then she didn't know what was.

With a nonchalance she didn't feel, Gwen unzipped the skirt and let it fall to the floor. Well, she had to help it fall a little bit, but once the waistband squeezed past her hips, the skirt pooled around her feet and she stepped out of it.

"There." She shrugged. "It's just me again. Plain ole Gwen."

"I like plain ole Gwen." His eyes never leaving hers, Alec advanced toward her, shirttails flowing behind him, deliberation in every step.

Gwen saw everything in slow motion—the purposeful stride, the swing of his arms, the play of muscles across his chest and the heat in his gaze.

She had a major you-man-me-woman moment and barely kept from flinging herself at him and moaning, "Take me now!" What she did say was, "Alec, you don't have to pretend. I understand, and you won't hurt my feelings." A nice little lie for the record because her feelings were jumping around waving signal flares. Over here! Over here! Good to go!

"I think we're way beyond pretending, aren't we, Gwen?"

She felt like a hawk's prey must feel. Gwen stomped on the skirt, just in case it was still active, or something.

It didn't matter.

"Alec!" She snapped her fingers. "Wake up." Gwen kicked the skirt under the coffee table.

It didn't matter because Alec now stood in front of her. Stood *very* close. And the way he looked at her, claiming her and offering himself at the same time, well, a man didn't look at a woman that way unless he was prepared to act on it.

Alec tugged gently at the hem of her sweater. "Maybe you should take this off, too, in case it got magnetized by the skirt."

"What?" Could that happen? Gwen tried to remember if anyone had said anything about such a possibility, but her brain wasn't working right.

Alec grasped both arms above her elbows and ran his hands up and down. "Need some help?" He leaned down and placed a light kiss at the point where her neck met her shoulder. Tingles raced over her body.

If she hadn't needed help before, she did now, because her arms were noodles and her legs were jelly and her brain was mush—she'd become a tray of hospital food.

She had to know for certain whether or not Alec was *truly* attracted to her and wasn't influenced by the skirt. So she crossed her arms and grasped the hem of her sweater, except taking off a sweater with noodle arms wasn't possible, so Alec, with his very strong unnoodlely arms helped her.

Then he reached behind her to unhook her bra. "The magnetism might have rubbed off on it," he murmured in the general vicinity of her jaw and earlobe, which he kissed gently as he spoke—a neat trick.

Gwen inhaled sharply and wondered if she ought to protest. But he did have a point. If there was the *slightest* chance that he was right, then she should dispense with her bra.

She allowed him to peel it off her.

He gave her a frank assessment. "You are a stunning woman."

"Is that stunning 'good,' or stunning 'bad'?"

"Can't you tell?"

She shivered at his hot look, which was odd, because a look of molten desire like that should have made her feel warm. Warm? Who was she kidding? She should have been burning, not shivering.

Of course, the shivering part could have come from the way Alec's fingers traced ever-narrowing circles over her skin and the way he concentrated on what he was doing.

She was thinking pretty hard about it herself, though she tried not to, since any moment, he'd probably realize what he was doing—or rather to whom he was doing it—and the spell would be broken.

And once it was, there would be the most incredibly awkward moments while he apologized and she rounded up all her clothes and—

"Alec...Alec, I still have on my underwear!"

"Patience, Gwen." He bent his head and trailed his lips behind his fingers.

Gwen swallowed and tried to remember to concentrate, though when she felt his tongue touch her skin, she felt like diving into a pool of sensual amnesia. But she had to be strong. She had to convince Alec how important it was that she take off her underwear.

"Alec, listen." She put both hands on either side of his face and lifted it from her chest. Looking into his eyes, she willed him to pay attention. "My panties were right next to the skirt. Maybe they were affected, too."

He blinked.

"They're proba_ ly why you're still finding me so irresistible."

They both looked down at her standard-issue beige panties.

"Then by all means, let's get rid of them," Alec said.

"But...but you might not find me attractive anymore."

He gazed into her eyes and she saw a little of the old Alec behind the desire. He put his hands over hers and pulled them away from his face. "Gwen, my friend, soon to be my very *good* friend—taking off your clothes generally won't make you unattractive to a man."

"But this is a special circumstance."

"That it is, Gwen, that it is." He slid his fingers beneath the elastic of her panties.

"Alec, would you do me a favor first?"

"I think that right now, I can guarantee you'll get pretty much anything you want."

She drew a deep breath. "Would you kiss me? I mean, you never have, not a real kiss, and, well, later, you might not want to."

He placed her hands on his shoulders, then looped his arms around her. "Gwen, I wanted to kiss you before you ever put on that skirt."

"Then why didn't you?"

"I was waiting for a signal."

"Hey, I'm standing here nearly naked—what are you waiting for now?"

At that, he pulled her to him, crushing her breasts against his bare chest.

Gwen nearly collapsed in an old-fashioned swoon and he hadn't even started kissing her yet.

He sighed and just held her tightly for several moments. "You feel so good in my arms."

Well, yes. However, "I hope that's not a euphemism for 'let's just be friends.'"

"Gwen!" Pulling back slightly, he gave a half chuckle, buried his hand in her hair, tilted her head and took her lips with his.

Kiss was such an inadequate word, Gwen decided. Because otherwise, how could the word kiss describe both Alec's teasing exploration and Eric's very good imitation of a wet vacuum cleaner?

Make that Eric's *excellent* imitation of a wet vacuum cleaner. After all, she had to give Eric his due.

And then she never had to think about him again because he was no longer the last man who'd ki—wetly sucked her face.

At first the sensations of finally kissing Alec were too much to process. She'd been longing for this for weeks, even though she'd at first pretended she didn't, then acknowledged that she did, but that it would never happen.

She was pretty sure the reality beat anything she'd imagined. Not exactly sure because so far, the reality was too intense.

Wave after wave of sensation rolled through her and Gwen just held on and surfed. She thought she might be getting the hang of it, when Alec lifted his mouth.

"You gonna kiss me back?"

Gwen heard him through a fog. "Wasn't I?"

"No."

"I—I...I guess I forgot."

"You...forgot?"

"Well, you were doing such a good job all on your own."

"Was I?" His gaze roamed over her face and he brushed her hair back over her shoulder.

"Yes," she said with a quivering sigh.

He smiled. "I can do better with feedback."

"There can be better?"

"Oh, yeah." He kissed her again, gently this time, lightly brushing her lips, coaxing a response from her.

The waves had become ripples. Nice ripples, but ripples all the same. Gwen wanted waves. Big, splashy waves.

So she opened her mouth and kissed him back.

Alec was right—it could get better.

For a minute, Gwen didn't think she could survive better. Then, she began to focus on the individual sensations, like the feel of Alec's lips, the taste of him and the way he held her tucked against his shoulder so that she felt completely surrounded by him and very much desired.

She moved her hands from their death grip on his shoulders and cupped the back of his head, burrowing her fingers in the soft crispness of his hair.

He took her lower lip in his mouth and tugged gently and she stood on tiptoe and did the same with his.

His hands, which had been splayed against her back, began moving in slow warming circles. Gwen liked the way his hands felt on her skin and thought she might like to feel her hands on his.

Abandoning his hair, she slipped her hands beneath his shirt and skimmed them over his back, investigating the muscles and feeling them bunch when his hands circled ever lower. And lower. And then he slipped them beneath the elastic and moved her panties lower, as well.

Gwen wiggled and shimmied. She felt him smile against her mouth and she smiled, too. When her panties got to her knees, she gave another shimmy and felt them fall. Without breaking the kiss—why would she want to do something stupid like that?—she stepped out of one leg and used the other to kick them in the general vicinity of the skirt.

There. She was totally and completely out from under the influence of the skirt and any ancillary powers it might have invested in her underwear.

Of course that meant she was totally and completely naked, too. The thought made her breathless. No, maybe it was Alec kissing her breathless. Or maybe it was the way he gripped her bottom and fit her closely against him, then rocked his hips. Yeah, that must be it. She forced herself to breathe, and not only because breathing rubbed her against the very interesting bulge in Alec's pants, but because she needed the oxygen. Really. Truly. Her breath came quicker. Yes, she sure needed a lot of that oxygen.

It sounded like Alec needed oxygen, too. In fact, the lack of clothes on Gwen's part didn't seem to be causing him to back off at all. If anything, if the movements of his tongue in her mouth and his hands kneading her bottom and holding it against his pelvis were valid indications, her nudity had only aroused him more.

Gradually, it occurred to Gwen's lust-soaked mind that any boost the skirt had given her, attractiveness-wise, had long since worn off and she was holding Alec's interest, among other things, all on her own.

A sudden jolt of realization zapped her, acting like the proverbial bucket of cold water.

She was naked in Alec Fleming's living room.

To be accurate, she was naked in his arms in his living room—his shirtsleeve-covered arms.

She pushed against him. "Hey! You're still wearing all your clothes!"

"I know." He grinned. "And I've never been more turned on in my life."

"Yeah?"

"Oh, yeah."

"Well, you know, you can be even more turned on." As she spoke, Gwen slipped his shirt off his shoulders.

"I don't see how."

"Take off your socks and shoes."

He hesitated, then kicked off his shoes. "Though I consider myself a fairly open-minded guy, the socks and shoes aren't doing it for me."

"It's not for you. It's for me. A guy naked except for his socks and shoes really dings the ick meter," Gwen told him. "So, by getting them off you now, I'm setting myself up for a really great visual later."

"Not too much later, I hope." Alec had ripped off his socks so fast, Gwen saw them land behind him before she knew they were gone.

"Ooo, a fast worker."

"Only when I should be."

"How very reassuring." Gwen kissed him and reached for his belt buckle, undoing it and the fastener at the waistband of his pants at same time.

She slowly and carefully eased down the zipper, trying not to think of that *very* unfortunate incident with Eric, who had still been wearing his socks and boots, but had inexplicably decided to forgo wearing briefs under his jeans that day.

She thrust her tongue deep into Alec's mouth and succeeded in banishing thoughts of Eric. Especially since there appeared to be so much more of Alec to get in the way of rogue zippers.

Gwen gave an anticipatory shiver before pulling off his pants and whatever he was wearing beneath them all at once.

Then she stepped back and got a very nice visual indeed.

She sighed and a flash of uncertainty crossed Alec's face. How utterly endearing.

"Didn't anyone tell you perfection is boring?" she asked and watched smugness replace the uncertainty.

"I could go put on a sock."

"Don't you dare."

He grinned. "I think it's time to let the cat out."

"I don't think I've ever heard sex called that before."

"I meant Armageddon."

"Gee. And the French just call it the 'little death.' Your term is so much more...promising."

"I'll show you promising. Stand back." He opened the door, stepped aside, and Armageddon raced out and headed for safety beneath the sofa, running right over the clothes he found in the way.

"*That* wasn't promising," Gwen said.

"Come here."

When she approached, Alec scooped her up in his arms and carried her over to the bed, kicking the door shut behind him.

"Nice move," she murmured.

"Call me a traditionalist." Slowly, he lowered her to the floor, sliding her down his body. As a move went, that was a pretty good one, too.

Alec turned the bedside lamp to low and peeled back the comforter.

"I'm a traditionalist in other areas, as well." He opened the bedside drawer and removed a handful of condoms.

"And an optimist." There must have been half a dozen at least.

"Just easing your mind."

Gwen checked the brand. "Oh, good. No ridges or pleasure nubs. I *hate* pleasure nubs." Eric had insisted.

There was laughter in Alec's voice. "Trust me. I don't need help from pleasure nubs."

Stretching out on the bed with him, Gwen marveled at her complete lack of self-consciousness. She had been naked for a while now, but they'd skipped right over that awkward part and it felt exactly right to be in Alec's arms.

He ran his finger along the curve of her hip. "Why did we ever think this would be a bad idea?" he asked, echoing her thoughts.

"Because we were friends?"

"Do we have to stop being friends?"

Only when it ends, Gwen thought. But she just shook her head as Alec gathered her to him, skin to skin, and kissed her.

He did a lot more things and Gwen couldn't ever remember laughing so much or having so much fun. Alec clearly savored being with her. When he stroked her and she responded, she could feel his pleasure as well as her own. And when something didn't work, he didn't take it as a personal affront to his technique. Of course, with Alec, most everything worked. He quickly adjusted the pressure of touch, always flirting with the line where teasing became torment.

But the best was the sheer pleasure in his expression. It inspired Gwen to keep it there.

With Eric, lovemaking had always been so deadly serious and...and Gwen had been guilty of faking it a time or two. Or three.

Okay, quite a lot, especially toward the end, but it was just easier that way. Eric had required so much coaching. She had had to keep up a running commentary of whether this was good or that felt better, and frankly, she would get confused about *what* she'd said *when* and would just want the whole thing over with.

Which should have been a clue that the relationship was over, except that Gwen had thought people put up with that sort of thing in long-term relationships. They called it working through problems.

There would be no problems with Alec in this area. Gwen knew that right off when she heard herself spontaneously purring and moaning and yessing and don't stopping and *ohmygaaawwwwdding*.

Alec's preferred method of feedback consisted of various inflections of her name. There was the, "Oh, Gwen," said very fast and the "Ohhhhhh, Gweeeen..." said really slow. She was rather partial to the "Oh, yes, Gwen, oh, yes" and the fervently whispered, "Hurry, Gwen!"

That last one had to do with recalcitrant condom wrappers and the fact that their hands were shaking so much neither could get the thing open until Gwen tried ripping it with her teeth and may or may not have punctured the contents.

It didn't matter because Alec had managed to open another one and now Gwen was the one whispering, "Hurry!"

Alec positioned himself above her and she thought she'd help things along a little by lifting her hips and scooting down to meet him at the same time he thrust forward.

The instant result surprised them both. They stilled, then Alec settled himself against her and laced his fingers through hers. He smiled into her eyes. Just before he began to move, he said softly, "Wow, Gwen."

And it was her favorite of all.

Later, there was another, "Wow, Gwen," followed by Alec draping a heavy arm over her waist and pulling her next to him and saying, "Stay and sleep, Gwen," as though she planned to go anywhere.

Her last thought as she drifted to sleep was that she could stay here forever.

The next morning—or later that morning, almost noon, actually—Gwen woke first and stretched.

Looking across the pillow at Alec, she saw the dark

stubble in his jaw and felt several areas of her skin that were sensitive because of it. Some areas that made her blush, actually.

Moving quietly, she got out of bed and searched the kitchen for breakfast. Cold cereal and milk seemed to be about the extent of Alec's culinary supplies.

Gwen was in a muffin and scrambled eggs mood. And maybe strawberries, even though they weren't in season. She'd just pop over to her apartment and get a few things and Alec could wake up to warm muffins— or something else, depending on the timing.

Gwen rounded up her clothes, smiling as she slid on the skirt. "Good job," she told it.

GWEN WASN'T IN BED when Alec woke up, but he could hear her in the kitchen.

Oh, wow. He stretched, feeling muscles that hadn't been used in a very long while, and smiled. Burying his hands underneath his pillow behind his head, he stared up at the ceiling.

So this was it. The big *L*.

He'd been told he'd know it when it happened, which he'd dismissed as a blowoff answer. Funny how it turned out to be just that simple. Or complicated. Except this was Gwen and complicated meant good because he'd never be bored.

Love had snuck up on him. He couldn't pinpoint the exact moment he'd fallen in love with her. He was pretty sure it had been before last night.

And speaking of last night...Alec closed his eyes and relived several really outstanding moments. Gwen taking off her skirt right in his living room—that had been pretty outstanding. Yeah, Gwen definitely was the one for him. She was the woman for whom he'd gladly give up all other women because they no longer held any interest for him. He was going to spend all his time getting to know this one, figuring out what made her tick and letting her do the same for him.

He tried to imagine going back to his old life without her and couldn't. In fact, he was slightly nauseated at the thought of no more Gwen. Or maybe that was hunger. He wondered what she was doing out there in the kitchen and when she was going to come back in here and see if he was awake. And when she got close enough to the bed, he'd grab her and they'd let whatever she was cooking burn.

Maybe then, he'd tell her he loved her.

WHAT WAS SHE DOING?

Gwen stared at the muffins she'd just taken out of the oven. *Muffins.* Homemade. From scratch.

She'd set the table. She'd gone to the store and paid way too much for strawberries because they were romantic. She'd cooked an omelet with more egg whites than egg yolks because it was healthier. She'd washed dishes, some of which were left over from Alec's dinner last night. And most telling of all...*she'd started a load of laundry and had flung some of his things in with hers.*

Communal laundry. The thin edge of the wedge.

Gwen looked at the kitchen bar, which she'd set with actual cloth napkins...she was doing it again. Call it genetic encoding, her mother's influence or plain old nesting, but Gwen was catering to the man in her life once more. She didn't seem to be able to help herself.

But this is Alec, said a little feminine voice that sounded as though it were choking in pink lace. *He's worth it.*

Gwen's shoulders sagged. Yes, he was. That's why she wouldn't be able to help herself.

This relationship with Alec had temporary written all over it. Eventually, he'd go back to his real home and his real life and she'd be left behind. She'd be hurt—that was a given—and she would have wasted all that time and energy pandering to him, ending up back where she began with nothing more than some really great memories.

She had great memories now. Why not skip the wasted time and the hurt?

It wasn't too late. She could go out with the flourish of this great breakfast, pack up that stupid skirt and mail it off to Kate. Then she'd get back on track with her plan to impress her boss, get a promotion, then a personal assistant and thus achieve success and eternal happiness.

And *then*, if Alec were still—no. No false hopes. He definitely wouldn't be around.

Quietly, Gwen fixed a plate for him, leaving him all the muffins, then wrote him a breezy "hey let's do this again sometime" note. Why burn bridges?

Well, she wasn't *perfect*.

12

BUT SHE WAS a coward, which was why Gwen asked her mother to come over and help her prepare her kiosk ideas presentation.

Suzanne arrived armed with plots and strategies and her own notebook computer. Where Gwen had researched data, her mother had researched people. She had a file with more information on Gwen's boss than Gwen had learned in four years.

"And I'm playing tennis with Anna Gerald on Monday. We'll play doubles with Carol Hofner and her partner."

"Hofner as in Mrs. Robert Hofner? My boss's boss?"

"Of course. That's the point."

Gwen opened and closed her mouth. Her mother had a connection to *everybody*.

"I'll be talking you up to them, so be sure and look sharp Tuesday. I'll call and brief you on Monday night." She typed a calendar reminder entry, then sat back.

"Now pretend I'm your boss. Present your idea."

Her mother was a tough audience. Gwen was on her third time through when Alec arrived. She'd been expecting him, so it was a relief to finally get the "morning after," or more accurately, "afternoon after," face-to-face over with.

Gwen opened the door wide, so he could see that her mother was there.

Alec gave Gwen a long, silent, chastising look, then smiled over her shoulder. "How's it goin', Suze?"

Suze. Gwen tried not to cringe.

"Alec, is that you? Gwen, let the man in."

Without so much as a glance at her, Alec walked in.

"I've missed you at Fletchers," her mother said and raised her cheek for a kiss.

Alec obliged as though he and her mother had been on cheek-kissing terms for ages. "Gwen and I were there just last night, weren't we, Gwen?"

"Uh-huh." Boy, was he mad. Gwen hadn't anticipated that he'd be angry. If anything, she thought his ego might be bruised, but, truly, she'd expected him to think about it and be relieved.

"Gwen and I are brainstorming her kiosk campaign. Has she mentioned it to you?"

Alec sat on the sofa next to her mother, leaving Gwen standing awkwardly. "That's the very reason I'm here."

"It is?" Gwen asked.

He wouldn't even look at her.

Suze prepared to type notes. "Oh, good. Tell me your thoughts."

Alec leaned forward. "The kiosk idea is sound, but partnering with a snack food company would make it better. The point is to increase name recognition. With a partner, building costs would be shared, traffic would be increased and the advertising impact would be the same."

Shouldn't he be telling this to *her?*

"Excellent," said her mother, busy typing. "We'll incorporate that point into Gwen's presentation."

"Well, yeah, that would be great." Gwen tried to keep the sarcasm out of her voice. "But I'm hardly in a position to go find a company willing to partner with Kwik Koffee. Besides, I don't have the authority."

"No, but you have me." Alec gave her a direct look and she decided it was better when he wasn't meeting her eyes. "I'll introduce you to my grandfather." He glanced over at Suze and added, "Fleming Snack Foods."

"Oh, ho!" Gwen's mother literally clapped her hands together. "Let me update my contact files. *A-l-e-c*..."

"Fleming," Gwen said slowly. "You're Fleming Snack Foods?"

"Yes." He gave her a puzzled look. "You knew that."

"Well, I knew your name and that your family was in the vending machine business, but I—I never realized..." Holy cow. Fleming Snack Foods. *Fleming Snack Foods.* They were huge. Giant. Almost a monopoly.

"Gwen, with connections like Alec, you don't need me. I'll concentrate on the Kwik Koffee end." Suze packed up her stuff.

"Mom, you're not leaving!"

"Yes." She indicated Alec. "You two need to talk."

He regarded her blandly. Gwen wasn't fooled. She was in such trouble.

She followed her mother to the door. "Mom!" she whispered. "Please stay."

"Gwen, I realize children think their parents are ancient, but I saw the way that man looked at you—is still looking at you, lucky girl. You also have an impressive case of beard burn. More than that is none of my business."

"Mom!"

"Go meet his grandfather." And she left.

Gwen turned to face Alec.

He pulled her note out of his pocket and tossed it on the table. "Explain this." His voice was diamond hard and his gaze was laser sharp.

"It's self-explanatory." She met his gaze defiantly.

To her surprise, his expression softened. "You're scared."

"Am not."

"Did I dream last night?" His voice had become low and husky.

She shook her head.

"Well?"

"Look, Alec, we both know it wouldn't work. Now especially."

"Why now 'especially'?"

"You're Fleming Snack Foods!"

"I work there, or did. And probably will again. So what?"

He was right. She was just making stupid excuses to cover up the real issue for her. Gwen cut through to the heart of the matter. She owed him that. "Did you enjoy your breakfast?"

"I would have enjoyed it more if you'd shared it with me."

"I don't want to do that every morning."

"Then don't."

"But...something *makes* me. I...lose myself in relationships. I sacrifice *my* goals and dreams and—"

"Whoa. Gwen, they were only muffins. Tasty, but a muffin is a muffin. Fleming makes them, too, you know. If you want, I can get you a discount. I'm not asking for any sacrifices, here."

"You don't have to ask. Men just expect—and get—them. I grew up with it and I do not want to end up like my mother."

"You could do a hell of lot worse."

"I could do a hell of a lot better. She did the corporate wife bit, living her whole life for my father and then he just walked out and left her with nothing. I'm not talking about money, I'm talking about the way of life she had. It depended on him. *He* got the promotions, the paycheck and the glory. She got nothing. I'm not going to make that mistake."

"But—"

"I know avoiding relationships seems extreme, but I can't seem to change any other way."

He drew a breath and Gwen could see that he was struggling to see her point of view. "So you're never going to marry and have a family?"

"Not until I do this for me first."

"*This* meaning your promotion?"

"Or the equivalent, yes."

Regarding her steadily, he asked, "Are you attaching any conditions to your promotion? For instance, do you have to do this by yourself or can you have help?"

"Help is fine."

"And how big a promotion?"

"Personal assistant big. I want a personal assistant. No other conditions."

"Gwen, I could hire you a personal assistant."

"No!"

"So there *are* conditions."

"I have to earn one—the kind of life that needs one."

"And once you achieve it, what then?"

"Then I'll be ready for a relationship." Her assistant would take care of all life's minutiae. "But I'm not going to flatter myself that you'll wait around for me."

Alec stood. "You're damn right."

That hurt. A lot. Even though she had no right to be hurt. Even though she was being grown-up and practical, the impractical little girl in her wanted him to gather her close and say, "Gwen, my dearest darling, I'll wait forever."

"I don't do waiting unless I have to," Alec informed her. "I'm going to expedite this entire situation. You want a promotion, we'll get you a promotion. Sunday dinner, with my family. You'll make your pitch to my grandfather."

Gwen stared at him. "You'd do that for me?"

"It's for me, too." He gave her a wry grin. "Do you think your boss would be interested in a joint venture with Fleming Snack Foods?"

"Interested? He'll wet his pants."

"That'll seriously weaken his negotiating position. Now, I'm going to leave you alone, because you've got a little over twenty-four hours to prepare. I'll warn you, my grandfather can be intimidating, but he's smart and shrewd and you've got a good idea. Make sure you've got the facts to back it up."

"Okay." Gwen was a little dazed.

"One more thing." Alec picked up her note and carefully ripped it three times, then sprinkled the pieces on her coffee table. "Now, kiss me goodbye and get to work."

He was bullying her.

And she didn't mind a bit.

BY ALL RIGHTS, Gwen should be more nervous than he was, except Alec knew how much he had personally riding on the outcome of this evening.

Gwen was, he decided, The One. Only she didn't want to be The One. Alec never thought he'd find The One without the woman realizing she was The One. In fact, he'd always thought the woman would have to inform him that she was The One. Kind of like Stef, only she was so *not* The One it wasn't funny.

His heart had nearly stopped beating when he'd read that awful note. He couldn't believe Gwen had baked muffins and then written a note like that. Not the Gwen he knew.

He'd felt...used. He was certain there was poetic justice in there somewhere, except that he'd never deliberately treated a woman that way.

Anyway, it didn't matter now that he understood what was driving her. He didn't have a problem with her need to accomplish something before committing to a relationship. His problem came with how long it was going to take her without his grandfather's cooperation.

"Take the next left."

Gwen was driving. He wished she'd say something.

She drove into the circular drive and stopped in front of his grandparents' stately brick home. Several other cars were already there. "I should have known your family would live in River Oaks."

He wished she'd said something else. "So they're rich. I'm not going to apologize."

They got out of the car. "Why should you apologize?" Gwen asked.

"For intimidating you."

"Oh, please. You've seen my folks' home. I'm hardly from the wrong side of the tracks."

"I know, so what's wrong with them living in River Oaks?"

"It would be easier to sell my idea if they were a little hungrier, that's all."

Alec ushered her up the front steps. "Don't worry. My grandfather has been plenty hungry and he doesn't forget."

Just before he rang the bell, he added, "You look great, by the way." She was wearing a red jacket and a black skirt.

"I know. I'm wearing the skirt."

Which explained his coughing fit as his grandmother opened the door.

Once he recovered, Alec introduced Gwen.

His grandmother had taken both Gwen's hands in hers. "I am *so* delighted to meet you, my dear."

"Is Alec here with the gel, yet?" sounded an accented voice.

Still holding Gwen's hands, his grandmother answered, "Yes, Liam."

"Will she do?"

"I believe so." His grandmother squeezed Gwen's hands and let go.

A short, white-haired, blue-eyed man appeared in the foyer and made a beeline for Gwen.

"Hi, Granddad. This is Gwen."

"Got yourself a real looker, did you, boy?" His grandfather stared at Gwen, who stared right back.

"Gwen is here to present the business proposal I told you about," Alec reminded him.

His grandfather snorted. "Whatever you say, boy. Let's eat."

Alec looked at Gwen, but she appeared more amused than offended. Well, give her time.

Unfortunately, she didn't need much time at all. The greeting in the foyer turned out to be the best part of a disastrous evening.

His mother immediately began interviewing Gwen about her people and, as it turned out, had already met Gwen's parents, which didn't surprise Alec at all. Once Gwen's lineage had been found to be acceptable, she was subjected to an all-out interrogation until at last, it was time to eat.

"A toast to the fair Gwen!" His grandfather raised his glass as they sat down. "May she prove the making of young Alec."

Young Alec glared around the table. Everybody was there. His parents, his uncle, his brother and sister and their spouses, his cousins, the kids, everybody. It was now embarrassingly clear that they'd misunderstood the reason he'd called them together. Alec tried to set them straight. "Gwen works for Kwik Koffee, so she understands the vending business."

His grandfather beamed. "Excellent! She'll do fine by you, then."

"She has some ideas for expanding the market," Alec tried again. "She's brought some interesting data with her."

His grandfather chuckled like an indulgent Santa Claus. "You didn't have to do that, gel."

"Yes, I did," Gwen said calmly. "Otherwise, you would be unable to make an intelligent business decision."

On second thought, maybe that wasn't calm. Maybe that was irritation. Certainly Alec was irritated.

"So how did you two meet?" asked Alec's mother.

"Alec moved to the apartment complex where I live while he's starting his business."

His brother snickered. "And how's that going, buddy?"

"Fine." Alec wasn't going to discuss the status of his mobile fitness center because he didn't want to draw attention away from Gwen's proposal. This meant he'd endure more heckling from his brother and cousins, but, hey, if all went well, it would be worth it.

But Gwen stood up for him. "It's going great! He's got the prototype of the exercise machine built and it's in the testing phase."

His cousin commented from the far end of the dining table. "Guess we'll have to start looking for your name on the Fortune 500."

This prompted another round of snickering until their grandfather spoke. "Alec doesn't have to spend time with that nonsense anymore now that he's brought us Gwen. I've always said that successful men are married men. They've got more at stake."

"They've got more distractions, too," Alec said.

"Now, Alec, you're smart, and the only thing that's been holding you back is that you've been too slow in settling down."

This was news to Alec and unfortunately, it caught him off guard.

"With a good woman like Gwen behind you," his grandfather nodded toward her "who knows how far you'll go?"

"Here, here!" said Alec's father, and raised his glass.

Had somebody written a script with absolutely the worst possible things to say from Gwen's standpoint?

One look at Gwen's face and Alec knew this had to stop. He stood and looked up and down the table. Silence fell. His mother gripped his father's hand. With a leaden feeling in his stomach, Alec realized they thought he was about to make an announcement. Well, he was. "Gwen is not here as my future wife. You all have misunderstood and it is making both of us uncomfortable. She is here, at my request, because she has a business proposition that I feel you should hear. That is all."

And he sat back down.

GWEN EXPERIENCED a variety of emotions as she stared at her plate. Hearing Alec emphatically protest that she was not his future wife hurt when it shouldn't have. Get over it, she told herself.

Naturally, his family would want a corporate wife for Alec the way her mother had been for her father and the way every woman present was. Even Alec's sister was a stay-at-home mom. Granted, all the kids were at the preschool age, but still. And no surprise that Alec would want to please his family. It made sense. But she couldn't be a corporate wife. Not even for Alec.

But he hasn't asked you, has he?

Because he knows I'd say no.

Would you?

"Yes!" Gwen said aloud and then noticed everyone was looking at her. "The...the cranberry sauce. It's the whole berry kind. My favorite."

"The chutney is a family recipe," Alec's grandmother said into the silence. "You must let me give it to you."

The rest of dinner was subdued. And afterward, they all listened politely and took copies of her lovely charts and pretty graphs and location studies and rents and all the rest.

But they were only being polite.

"I'm sorry," Alec apologized the instant they were out the door.

"I'm sorry, too," Gwen said. Actually she was kind of numb. She'd foolishly pinned her hopes on Alec's grandfather and he'd only been interested in her as a potential wife for Alec.

"But I'm more sorry." Alec held out his hand for the keys and opened the car door for her. "Because I know the corporate-wife thing is your nightmare life and you're thinking that's the kind of wife I need or I'll suffer some way, but that's not you, so you're going to walk away from all that utterly fantastic sex."

Gwen laughed in spite of herself. "I was thinking about my presentation. I wasn't thinking about the sex."

He bent close to the window and murmured, "How could you forget the sex? It was great. If you're having short-term memory problems, hey, I'll be glad to give you a refresher any time."

"Stop trying to make me laugh."

"You're taking this too seriously."

"And you're not." She sighed. "You heard what they said about you settling down."

"I don't care what they said!"

"You care." She waited while he walked around to the driver's side and got in. "You care so much that you were willing to turn your life upside down for months while you recreated your grandfather's early struggle in this country. And, be truthful—you haven't broken the rules once, have you?"

"Well, New Year's and the tux—"

"You bought it used."

"All right, then no. I've played it straight."

"And I admire you for it," Gwen told him sincerely. "But those aren't the actions of a man who bucks his family."

"Gwen, I set a goal and am meeting a challenge because I find it interesting and reenergizing, if you will. If I were doing it solely for their approval, I wouldn't be getting such a kick out of it. And if I don't seem like a man who bucks his family, it's because until tonight, I haven't had reason to buck."

"And you still don't," Gwen said firmly, ignoring

her whiny inner voice. "Because I have other plans for my life."

He was silent for a few moments, then said quietly, "Maybe I do, too."

RUMORS WERE FLYING on Monday as the Kwik Koffee corporate hierarchy arrived and secreted themselves with upper-level management. Gwen was frustrated when her boss, with the other regional directors, was closeted in meetings in the morning, then gone all afternoon taking the big shots around to meet the major clients. It was probably just as well, since Gwen's mother was playing tennis with Mrs. Hofner. Gwen didn't know how much good that would do for her career, but at least it kept her mother out of salsa bars.

On Tuesday morning, Gwen, as instructed, wore a severe navy blue suit with a red blouse. Her mother had reported that Mrs. Hofner was full of talk about the big meetings and that heads would roll unless there were some changes. This was nothing Gwen couldn't have figured out for herself, but it was interesting to hear another perspective.

Gwen heard her boss arrive and was startled to be called into his office moments later. Norman Eltzburg smiled at her. Beamed, actually. The expression looked unnatural on him.

Gwen eyed him suspiciously.

"Bob Hofner had an interesting call yesterday," he began.

Oh, no. What had her mother done?

"It seems Liam Fleming, himself, called Harry Le-Breaux."

Alec's grandfather had called the head of Kwik Koffee! Gwen's heart picked up speed. She'd thought he'd ignored her presentation.

"LeBreaux called Hofner and Hofner called me. I had no idea you were dating the grandson of the Fleming Snack Foods founder. Very clever of you."

Gwen decided not to correct him.

"Fleming has put an attractive proposal on the table."

"They have?"

"Yes. Freestanding kiosks featuring their product and ours."

"You mean he liked my idea?"

"Your—" Mr. Eltzburg chuckled. "Well, yes, Fleming did mention that you'd brought him some data." He shuffled a few papers on his desk and Gwen saw her charts and graphs. "Good work, Gwen. You made the most of an opportunity and I want you to know that Kwik Koffee appreciates your initiative. You probably should have approached me first, but don't worry. Now that I'm up to speed, I can take it from here."

"Take what?"

"Well, Gwen, I understand that you'll be busy with wedding plans—"

"*What?*"

"And I don't want there to be a break in continuity when you resign."

Gwen had expected to be presenting her plan herself, not denying wedding rumors. "I am not getting married and I'm not going to resign."

"It's okay, Gwen. I know you have to say that until

things are official." He winked—winked!—at her. "However, we would like for you to attend the meeting this morning. The Flemings will be there and it'll make a nice show of support."

"I'm not getting married!"

He held a finger to his lips. "I know. I won't say a word to anyone, except I hope you'll allow me to express my very best wishes for your future happiness."

Gwen was livid. Alec's grandfather was determined to see her as nothing more than future Fleming breeding stock. Yet he thought enough of her idea to bring it to Kwik Koffee without telling her. And now her boss was stealing it.

Her idea.

Gwen stormed back to her cubicle and did what any woman in her situation would have done. She called her mother.

Suzanne let her vent for about two minutes, then interrupted crisply. "That's enough. Shake it off. Gwen, this is a typical hostile business move on your boss's part. You're a threat to him. The wedding talk was only a smoke screen. Fleming is using it to catch Kwik Koffee off balance and your boss is doing the same thing to you. You are going to go to that meeting and you are going to fight for recognition."

"How?" Gwen asked wearily.

"Oh, ye of little faith. I have spent my entire married life negotiating waters filled with corporate sharks. I've helped your father outmaneuver more blatant power grabs than this. I'm on my way."

"Thanks, Mom."

"And Gwen? *Is* there any truth to the wedding talk?"

"*No!*"

"Do you want there to be?"

"Yes," Gwen admitted. Wanting Alec was never an issue. Allowing herself to have him, was. "Except that he needs someone like you. And I can't be you, Mom."

"Has he *asked* you to be me?"

"Actually, he hasn't asked me to be anything at all."

"Have you given him the chance?" Suzanne asked shrewdly.

"No," Gwen said in a very small voice. No, she'd written a note, then brought her mother in as a buffer, then declared that she had to achieve corporate success before deigning to consider a relationship.

"Don't you think you should?"

Gwen dropped her head to her desk. "He won't. I told him I had other plans for my life."

Her mother sighed. "Well, it's going to be full morning, but we can deal with that, too."

It was only after her mother hung up that Gwen began having second thoughts. Had she really tacitly agreed that her mother was going to deal with Alec? What had she been thinking? Gwen was about to call her back when the phone rang.

"Gwen!" It was Laurie. "There's a rumor going round that you're going to marry Fleming Snack Foods!"

ONCE HE'D GOTTEN past Gwen as a future Fleming wife, his grandfather had gone for her idea as Alec had known he would. It was similar to one they'd considered, but had rejected because they hadn't wanted to get into the coffee arena. A joint venture with a coffee vending company made a lot of sense and the Kwik Koffee brass was practically blubbering with delight.

Alec would have liked to have been there when Gwen told her boss, but being at this meeting would be nearly as good. Once she got her promotion—and she surely would—well, then he'd convince her she was perfect for him.

He enjoyed watching her standing at the head of the table by the overhead projector. Earlier, her boss had tried to take over, but Gwen had neatly undercut him by offering to present updated figures that her boss didn't have. She'd approached the front and once she was there, she stayed. It was clear that this was, and had been, her baby from start to finish.

Alec had had a long talk with his grandfather about Gwen, the kind of woman she was and his feelings for her.

Then he'd resigned from Fleming Snack Foods. Even Gwen would realize that he wouldn't need a corporate wife if he wasn't a corporate executive. But that wasn't the reason Alec had quit. He liked being his own boss and he wanted to stay that way. His ten-minute exercise idea had potential and he wanted to see it through.

"You don't mind if I hire *her* to replace you, do you?" the old man whispered now.

"Do whatever you want. It'll be her decision."

His grandfather regarded him thoughtfully. "Sometimes, a woman needs a man to tell her how it's going to be."

"I'll remember that," Alec murmured.

The lights had come up and Gwen was fielding questions now.

"Gwen, what's your background with this company?" one of the visiting Kwik Koffee corporate execs asked.

"She's been with us five years, four of those as my assistant," Norman Eltzburg inserted, obviously trying to regain some of his lost stature. "She shows a lot of potential."

"I already manage four district accounts and they were the only ones to show increased profits in your region," she pointed out.

Go, Gwen, Alec thought.

Eltzburg glared at her.

"Gwen did bring Fleming to the table," Mr. Hofner mentioned. "And in view of her future connection with that family, I think it's entirely appropriate for her to manage the project."

"I agree completely," Alec's grandfather said.

Alec wished he hadn't.

Gwen drew herself up and spoke crisply. "There is a rumor that Alec Fleming and I are engaged. That is not true. Right, Alec?" She looked to him for confirmation.

Wrong he wanted to say. "That's correct, gentlemen."

But at Gwen's next words, he wished he hadn't agreed.

"So any project I undertake will command my total attention for as long as I'm involved."

She was prepared to play the part of the consummate corporate drone—prepared to give up any personal life and work ninety hours a week. *And she was looking forward to it.*

Alec's heart sank. At that moment, he knew that even if Gwen were offered the project and with it a promotion and the personal assistant she wanted so much, she would be completely and wholly involved in it. No matter what she'd said earlier, there wouldn't be time for any kind of relationship, let alone marriage.

Well, if that's the life she thought would make her happy, then let her have it. "Excuse me," he whispered to his grandfather. "I have an appointment."

He actually did, but he didn't have to leave for an hour and he couldn't stand what Gwen was doing a moment longer.

His grandfather reached over and squeezed his arm in mute sympathy. Alec offered a lopsided smile and slipped out the side entrance.

OH, GREAT. He was leaving just when they were getting to the good part. He wasn't supposed to leave. She and her mother hadn't discussed Alec leaving. She stared hard at his back, hoping he'd turn around as he went out the door.

He didn't.

"Gwen, as far as we're concerned, this project is yours," one of the brass said. Gwen had forgotten his name, but she was certain her mother hadn't.

"Now, we'll need to discuss when you can get a report on—"

"No. Thank you," she added.

"What?" Everyone stared at her.

"I appreciate your offer, but—" She drew a deep breath. "The project I'm going to be working on isn't with this company."

There was silence in the room. As one, heads swiveled to Alec's grandfather.

"Don't look at me. But I would have hired her. Smart gel."

Gwen beamed at him.

"About some things," he added.

"Don't worry," she told him. "I'm smart about other things, too."

Mr. Hofner cleared his throat. "Gwen, naturally, there would be a substantial rise in salary as commensurate with your increased responsibilities. That's understood."

She wasn't even tempted. "Thank you, again, but no. I never thought I'd say this, but my decision isn't about money. I'm going to be working with a start-up company." Trust her mother to figure out a way to combine business and pleasure. By working with Alec, Gwen could satisfy her need to achieve *and* her need to cater to the man in her life. She *really* wished the man she wanted in her life was here to hear this.

"But, Gwen, you haven't heard our offer." Mr. Hofner still looked stunned.

"Speaking of offers...I'm late for an interview with the owner now."

As Gwen walked by Alec's grandfather, he said, "Hurry, gel. He walks mighty fast."

Gwen grinned and practically ran from the room.

Her mother intercepted her outside the conference

room door. "He's down in the atrium staring at the fountain."

"Thanks, Mom."

Her mother gave her a thumbs-up.

Had the elevators ever been so slow? Gwen burst into the lobby and headed for the stone benches surrounding the water wall, a popular spot for workers to eat their lunches.

Fortunately, it wasn't lunchtime and Alec was alone. Or he was alone until Gwen sat down next to him.

"Hi."

He didn't look at her. "Did you get your promotion?"

"They offered it to me."

"Congratulations."

"Thanks. It felt great. I'd reached my goal. So then I quit."

He turned to stared at her in surprise. "Why?"

"I told them I was going to work for a start-up company with a great concept—ten-minute exercise breaks for office workers."

A slow smile spread across Alec's face.

When he didn't say anything, Gwen poked him with her elbow. "My mother told me that I should expect a proposal at this point and so far, my mother has been right about everythi—"

Before she finished speaking, Alec had drawn her to him. "I've been trying to find the right time to tell you I loved you, but it just wasn't happening."

"This is a good time, because I love you, too. *And* I've quit my job, so I'm currently considering offers."

"Tell me that means you'll marry me."

She pulled back. "Well, are you asking?"

"No, I'm telling you how it's going to be."

"Okay." She'd let him get away with being dictatorial this once.

Especially since he was currently reminding her that he was an incredibly good kisser.

"You didn't have to quit your job," he said a few moments later.

"Yes, I did. It really made me mad the way your family didn't even want to hear about your exercise business. All they were interested in was whether you were going to marry the right kind of woman."

"I *am* going to marry the right kind of woman."

"And don't you forget it!"

Instead of laughing, he gave her a funny look. "I should tell you that I wasn't happy about the other night, either. And, well, I told grandfather that I wasn't coming back to the company."

"You mean you quit?"

Alec nodded.

"And?"

"I think he wants to hire you to take my place."

"He said something like that." Gwen laughed. "At least now he considers me as more than window dressing."

"You do know that I don't ever expect you to do the corporate wife drill."

"And I'm not going to—but can I still have a big, hunky diamond?"

"I'm poor, remember?"

Gwen grinned at him. "I'll wait."

THEY WENT BACK to Gwen's cubicle to start clearing out her things and found that Suzanne had commandeered Gwen's desk and phone.

"Oh, good, you're back. Alec, I have another name for you, in case your appointment with Bertie doesn't work out." Suzanne ripped off a piece of paper and handed it to Alec. "I've found a couple of potential backers for him," she explained to Gwen.

Gwen and Alec looked at each other. She knew exactly what he was thinking, because she was thinking the same thing.

"Hey, Suze, how would you like a job as an assistant in a start-up company for low pay and no benefits?" he asked.

"What's the company's name?"

Alec and Gwen looked at each other. "Don't know yet," Alec said.

"And what would I do?"

"Basically what you do now, Mom, only you'd get paid."

"But not much," Alec added.

Suzanne thought about it. "Could I be called Executive Assistant to the chairman and CEO?"

"Heck, we'll make you a vice president. Titles don't cost anything."

"Then, I accept." She beamed at Gwen. "Look at me, out in the work world!"

"Yeah. Dad should see you now."

Suzanne's happy expression evaporated and Gwen could have kicked herself for bringing up her father. "Actually, he will see me," her mother said. "He's coming back."

"He is?"

Near tears, Suzanne nodded. "That silly man was having bouts of high blood pressure and he was hiding it from me."

Gwen gripped Alec's arm. "Is he going to be okay?"

"Yes. He'd been told to reduce stress and slow down and he thought I'd be disappointed in him if he couldn't work as hard. So he quit and went off by himself. Can you imagine?" She sniffed.

"Well, it's good that Dad's coming back, because—" Gwen grinned up at Alec and he nodded "—we're getting married!"

"Yes!" In an emotional about-face, Gwen's mother enveloped them both in a hug. "Though I'm not surprised. All right. Enough of this." She shooed them away from Gwen's desk. "Let me just start a couple of files and then I'll check my contacts and see what kind of a deal I can get on office space. Alec, you'd better get ready for your appointment. Oh, and Gwen? We've got to decide on a date for the wedding..."

Gwen was absolutely not ready to discuss weddings with her mother. She threw a panicked look at a grinning Alec. "I'm going with you!"

They slipped out while her mother was on the phone. Gwen figured she'd pack up her stuff later. Or maybe her new personal-assistant vice president mother would.

Alec pressed the button on the elevator. "You know, Gwen, my appointment isn't for another forty-five minutes."

"Great!" The elevator arrived and they stepped inside. "We've got time for lunch."

"Or not." Without warning, Alec placed both hands

on either side of her face and drew her into a kiss of breathtaking intensity.

How had she thought she could live without this? Without him?

"Who needs lunch?" she asked, and kissed him back.

_____Epilogue_____

GWEN COULD hardly believe that she was a Valentine bride. She and Alec had barely become used to the idea of being engaged when Suzanne discovered that due to a cancellation, she could get a huge discount on a wedding reception if they were willing to get married on Valentine's Day.

They decided to go for it and now, less than two months after Chelsea had thrown the skirt to Gwen, Gwen stood in a fairy princess wedding dress with her new husband on the balcony at the Old Bayou Inn and prepared to throw her bouquet and the skirt.

"So what's the holdup?" Alec asked. "I've been very good about all this wedding stuff, and now, I want my reward."

"You've been rewarded plenty lately."

"But never with a married woman. I've heard they're really hot."

"Only when the right man lights their fire."

"You should see the match I've got in my pocket. _Throw the damn bouquet._"

"But Kate's not down there!"

"So she'll miss out." He nuzzled the side of her neck. "Does that mean _I_ have to miss out?"

"Alec! I have to throw the skirt to her. It's her turn!" Gwen scanned the restless females crowded below her.

"Maybe I can throw the bouquet while we're waiting. Kate doesn't need to catch both."

Down in the crowd, she spotted Laurie.

"Come to mama!" Laurie called.

Gwen caught a glimpse of Brian looking on, grinned and tossed her the bouquet. There was a struggle— bouquet catchings were not for the timid these days— but Laurie emerged triumphant.

And just then, Gwen saw Chelsea dragging Kate through the crowd of disappointed females. If they only knew that the skirt held the real magic.

Nearly overcome with happiness—okay, and lust— Gwen kissed Alec, and then tossed the skirt toward her friend. "Your turn, Kate!"

Silhouette Books invites you to cherish
a captivating keepsake collection by

DIANA PALMER

They're rugged and lean...and the best-looking, sweetest-talking men in the Lone Star State! CALHOUN, JUSTIN and TYLER—the three mesmerizing cowboys who started the legend. Now they're back by popular demand in one classic volume—ready to lasso your heart!

You won't want to miss this treasured collection from international bestselling author Diana Palmer!

LONG, TALL
Texans

CALHOUN, JUSTIN & TYLER
(On sale March 2002)

Available at your favorite retail outlet.

Silhouette®
Where love comes alive™

PSLTT

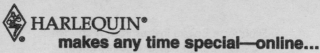